# SINGLE DAD FOR THE RUNAWAY BRIDE

## COURTNEY CLARK MICHAELS

AUGUST PUBLISHING

**Single Dad for the Runaway Bride**

by Courtney Clark Michaels

This book is a work of fiction. Names, characters, places and incidents are the product of the author's imagination or are used fictitiously. Any resemblance to actual events, locales, or persons living or dead is coincidental.



E book ISBN: 978-1-0670246-2-8

ISBN: 978-1-0670246-1-1

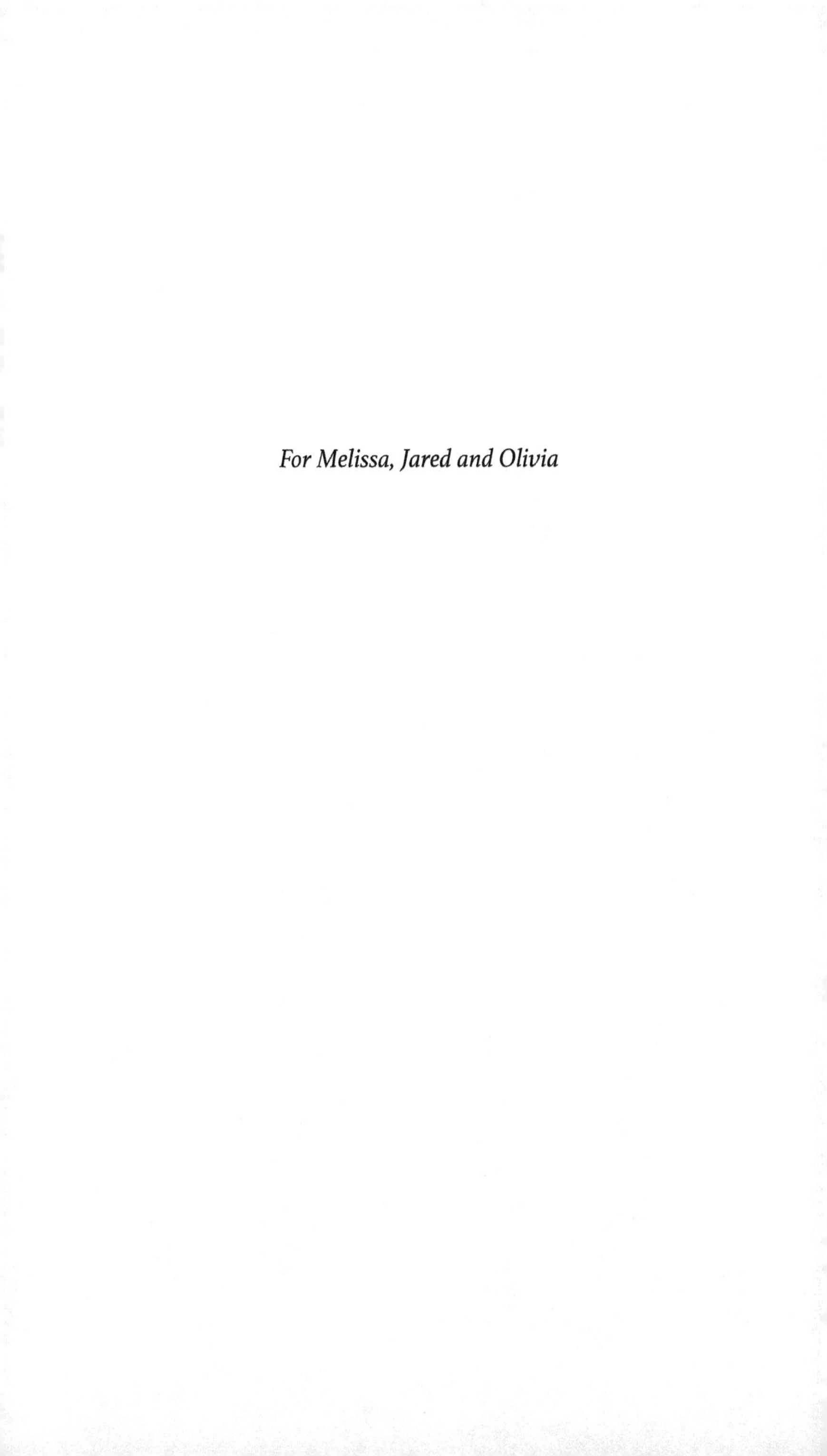

*For Melissa, Jared and Olivia*

# CHAPTER 1

The sun danced through the bridal suite, the scent of coconut and saltwater sang on the breeze, and Paige Beckett's bedazzled thong was beginning to chafe.

Not that she could do anything about it, not with two - *two* - pairs of control top underwear between it and her heavily beaded wedding gown. In Samoa, of all places! When the most she should be wearing on her way down to the beach was a bikini and a smile.

She closed her eyes and took a deep breath through her nose, then another. When she opened them, the view was the same. White-washed floorboards, pale aqua walls, bouquets of pink hibiscus on every sleek, modern surface and gauzy pale drapes that framed the powdered sugar shoreline and sparkling sapphire Pacific that stretched out towards the horizon. It was, without a doubt, the most romantic place Paige had ever visited. And she'd never been less comfortable.

Every sign of the three hours of preparation that Paige had undertaken was gone, a testament to the professionalism of the hair and makeup team The

Moananui Resort had provided. Not an errant bobby pin or false lash remained, the space having been ruthlessly cleared by the smiling glam squad before their departure. In fact, the bridal suite looked exactly the same as it had when she walked in yesterday, right down to her repacked suitcase by the bedroom door. The only sign five gregarious Samoan women had even been there was when Paige looked in the mirror. Her normally-tanned skin glowed, her green eyes looked luminous, and her hair– the colour a shade too platinum for a natural honey blonde, her colourist back home in New Zealand had pronounced – was twisted into an intricate updo that was a work of art itself. Their artistry, combined with the white and silver Art Deco-inspired trumpet gown her mother had insisted on buying for her had turned her from a simple country doctor to a glamazon. She even looked taller than her usual five and a half feet.

*I wish Mum hadn't insisted on underwear that matched the dress.*

Still, slight intimate discomfort was worth it to see her mother smile at the prospect of Paige's wedding. After several years of hints about settling down after beginning work as a doctor in her small hometown in the North Island, Paige had thoroughly embarrassed both of her parents by entering a reality dating show. She might have come out of *One True Love* with a fiancé in the show's hero Patrick Winslow, but Kathleen Beckett had condemned the notoriety regardless. It got even worse once the episodes aired and Paige realised that she had been edited to appear like a complete floozy - shots of her taking sips from her champagne glasses taken from different angles and playing in sequence, followed by clips of her wobbling on the spindly heels she'd repeatedly requested more comfortable replacements for had painted her as a torrid party girl, proving Kathleen's assertions that going on the show was a mistake. So if Paige had cast a wistful look at a simpler, flowing wedding gown in the bridal boutique while her mother fawned over the Gatsbyesque delight she currently wore, it was a small price to pay.

On the bed, her phone beeped. *Half an hour until the ceremony.* She'd be back in this room tonight as Mrs Paige Winslow, and the thought set butterflies loose in her stomach. She pressed her hands over her abdomen, breathing deep again.

*Nerves are normal. Nerves are normal.* She repeated the mantra in her head. That's all it was, nerves. It couldn't be the way Patrick ate his eggs on toast, cutting each piece of toast into nine squares and consuming them in a clockwise direction from the top right, leaving the centre square for last like a fucking psychopath. It couldn't be the way he squeezed the toothpaste tube from the middle, even though she'd told him it drove her nuts, or the way he'd handed her a daiquiri at the welcome dinner last night despite the fact she's specifically told him on one of their first televised dates she hadn't drunk rum since a particularly brutal episode in med school. Those weren't normal reasons to feel anxious. It was simply pre-wedding nerves, surely. Or perhaps the control-top underwear were finally crushing her diaphragm the way they had been threatening to since she wrestled them on.

Her alarm beeped again – the twenty minute warning the show producers had insisted she set. Outside of the walls of her medical practice, Paige was notoriously late. It drove Patrick crazy – he'd mentioned it several times in the two months they'd been conducting their relationship in secret since the show's filming wrapped in their native New Zealand. There was no way she was risking a lecture from him on their wedding day, especially with so many television cameras around.

Scooping up her room card and bouquet – the same bright pink flowers that adorned the bungalow's various tables – she took one last look in the mirror and headed for the door. There was a room closer to the beach ceremony location she was expected to wait in until the cameras were rolling. Paige had taken the walk that meandered through the lush tropical gardens, under traditional carved arches down to the ceremony site on the beach yesterday afternoon to ensure she was familiar with it, but there was nothing familiar about the way she felt as she walked the route now. The slap of her silver sandals seemed to echo on the stone pathways, a rhythmic beat leading her towards her future.

The thought caught in her mind and she stopped, reaching up to grasp one of the ornately carved arch supports as she swayed. It was cool in the shadow of the arch and Paige soaked in the brief respite from the heat, swallowing back the nerves – *it's just nerves* – that climbed her throat.

"Are you alright?"

Turning, Paige saw a young Samoan girl leaning against the next pillar, sipping a smoothie. Her hair was in two braids down her back and her dark, intelligent eyes were examining Paige curiously.

Paige offered her a weak smile. "I'm fine."

"You don't look fine." The girl's English was perfect. "You look like a princess."

Paige's smile grew, softened. "Thank you. That's very kind of you to say."

"Are you getting married today?"

"I am."

The little girl sighed deeply. "You're so lucky. I'm going to get married here, too."

"It's a good place to get married?"

"It's the *best* place to get married," Paige's new friend beamed at her. "All I need now is to meet my one true love, like you have."

Paige stilled, the phrase ringing in her ears. *One true love.* A slideshow of images flashed through her mind. The eggs. The toothpaste. The daiquiri.

Panic crawled up her throat, itchy and tight.

*It's fine*, she assured herself. *Nerves are normal.* Distantly it occurred to her that maybe this level of nerves wasn't quite run of the mill, but she pushed that thought aside. *Patrick.* She needed to see Patrick. He'd hold her hand and calm her down, that steady voice of his calming her the way he had when anxiety gripped her following the screening of the proposal finale, when comments had rolled in on her social media accounts calling her shitty names and telling her how Patrick would have been better off with the runner-up, Jacqui.

Paige forced a smile onto her face. "Do you know where I can find the Vainui Villa?"

The little girl nodded. "Come with me," she commanded Paige, and spun on her heel, striding off in the opposite direction, still sucking her smoothie through a straw.

Paige followed, lifting the front of her dress and sending up thanks that she hadn't caved to the producers' insistence on a fairytale train. Photographic it may have been, but it would also have hindered her significantly and her friend showed no signs of slowing down as she marched determinedly through bush-lined paths towards the room Patrick was sharing with his brother until he joined her in the bridal suite tonight.

The small villa came into view at last, a tasteful standalone structure with a wide porch that housed a glass-topped outdoor table, already scattered with a few empty beer bottles. Strangely, a bolt of confidence shot through Paige at the sight.

*Maybe he's nervous too.* Bolstered, she started up the porch steps, only to pause as her fiancé's voice reached her on the breeze.

"I wish there was a way to do it without marrying Paige," he was saying. "She's great to look at, but shit, she's boring. Jacqui would have been far more fun."

Horror washed over her, a bracing cold that almost brought her to her knees. The rushing in her ears almost drowned out the response.

"I know you feel that way, Patrick, but you have to be reasonable." *Natalia?* Natalia had been the producer on *One True Love*, always keeping an eye on the action, prodding it along even, with pointed questions and ruthless insinuations.

*Why is Patrick talking to her about this?*

"Paige was such a fan favourite," Natalia continued. "I know you preferred Jacqui, but you would have turned three quarters of the viewing audience against you. If you're looking at a career in entertainment after this, you need public approval on your side. Marry Paige and you can sign your own payslips with media endorsements and appearances."

Patrick sighed. "You're sure it will only be two years?"

"Two years, max." Natalia's voice was a firm birdlike chirp. Paige hated birds. "We'll engineer a separation and set you up with interviews that make you look like a heartbroken man bravely getting back out there. You'll be rolling in pussy and cash. Besides," the producer scoffed.

"She works so much you'll barely have to spend any time with her. I've never met anyone so dull in all my years doing this."

Nausea roiled through Paige, a sickly green that turned her vision black at the edges. Patrick had never wanted to marry her. He thought she was boring – *everyone* thought she was boring. The only unboring thing she'd ever done was enter the show and the consequences of that were closing in on her hard and fast as she tried to swallow back her shock.

*Fuck. Fuck. Fuck.*

She'd thrown away everything – her anonymity, her credibility, her parent's respect – to take a chance on love. And she wasn't enough.

The bouquet fell from her hands to the lush green grass as she turned and fled.

~

"I need a new room."

Mareko Osa didn't look up from the occupancy report he was studying as he lounged against the wall behind the front desk. He might have staked the entire future of his family on the success of The Moananui Resort, but room change requests were as common as coconuts and he had handpicked the finest customer service representatives from Samoa's islands to handle things like this.

"Is there a problem with your current room, ma'am?" Mareko heard Rachel, the current concierge, ask.

"No. However, I need another one. Right away. Any room will do." Panic crept into the woman's New Zealand accent now, a high-pitched thread that ran through the broad flat vowels.

There was a clack of keys and then a sympathetic noise. "I'm sorry, ma'am. I'm afraid we're fully booked."

"*Any* room," the foreign woman insisted. "A broom closet will do, if it's got a roll of paper towels I can use as a pillow."

"I really am sorry. There's nothing I can do," Rachel replied. "We're fully booked on account of... well... you know."

Mareko frowned at the slip in Rachel's professionalism, turning to shoot her a warning glance, but stopped when he saw the woman at the counter.

Blonde hair glowed in the shafts of light that streamed down into the open-air lobby, her green eyes almost otherworldly against the fresh dew of her rounded face. She looked like an angel.

*An angel in a wedding dress.*

The unexpected lust that had been building in him cooled like lava meeting the ocean.

The bride.

Mareko had personally worked to secure the filming of the wedding special of *One True Love* at The Moananui. He'd invested thousands in reinvigorating the already luxurious reception space and hired an additional team of gardeners to ensure the grounds were flawless. The income the publicity of appearing on the popular dating show would generate would set The Moananui up for years, securing his family's future. But that was reliant on the wedding taking place. A bride holding a sleek black suitcase and demanding a new room in the middle of his lobby ten minutes before the ceremony was due to start did not bode well.

"Can I be of assistance?" He rounded the reception desk, the occupancy report forgotten.

The bride – Paige Beckett, he recalled from the contract

negotiations – turned to face him and he almost stopped in his tracks as her eyes met his. The colour of emeralds, they would be arresting under any circumstances, but wide with dismay they fuelled every protective instinct in him. Mareko swallowed hard, pushing through the rising tide that thrummed in his blood, urging him to whisk her away and keep her safe. He hadn't studied in Paris and worked his way through luxury hotels in Geneva and Cairo only to find his own legacy, The Moananui, on the brink of financial ruin when he returned, to be swayed from his goals by a woman with eyes the colour of the lagoon's edge.

*Especially not one who's supposed to marry another man.*

"I'm afraid I need another room immediately," she said now, and Mareko worked to keep his expression neutral in response to the steel of her tone. Every exchange he had been party to with the *One True Love* producers had indicated that they felt the bride would be easily influenced, almost every detail of her wedding chosen by a committee of besuited executives and communicated to Mareko and his event planner without so much as a mention of the betrothed couple's preferences. In fact, he distinctly remembered a conference call in which the bride's insistence on choosing her own dress with her mother was met with the kind of eye-rolling indulgence of a parent when faced with a toddler tantrum.

"Rachel is correct," he replied. "We are fully booked tonight and tomorrow due to the production staff for the wedding."

She narrowed her eyes at him. "Fine. Then I would like a transfer to the airport."

Air left Mareko's body in a rush, alarm swooping in to take its place.

*Oh, that's not good.*

"Miss…"

"You do offer airport transfers, do you not?"

His brain raced, trying to work out a way around her request. He needed the wedding special to be filmed here on The Moananui Resort's expansive beachfront grounds. His *family* needed the wedding special to be filmed here. Maybe they didn't exactly know it, but his accountant sure as shit did.

Perhaps she was simply suffering from nerves. It wouldn't be the first time a matrimonial event had been at risk due to cold feet. Hell, he'd had them himself in the days leading up to his own marriage. He sometimes wondered even now what would have happened if he'd followed his gut and called off his wedding to Hélène. She might still be alive today.

As if summoned by his thoughts, a tiny hand slipped into his.

"What are you doing?"

Mareko closed his eyes briefly. "I am working, Rosa. Now is not a good time."

Paige smiled down at his daughter. "Now is the perfect time. It is lovely to see you again."

"Are you leaving?" Rosa gestured to Paige's suitcase. "What about the wedding?"

The bride grimaced. "Ah. Well, it turns out that Patrick was *not* my one true love. And I have you to thank for that, actually. If you hadn't helped me find him, I might not have realised."

Mareko turned to his daughter in disbelief, but she refused to meet his eyes.

"Now I'll head back to New Zealand and try again." Paige's smile tightened at the corners. "And you can have this, to remind you that true love is worth waiting for." She reached up and removed the sparkling headband that wrapped around her intricate hairstyle, pale ribbons trailing from the ends of the beaded length as she handed it over to Rosa who looked at it as if it were Britain's crown jewels.

This was bad. Cold feet were one thing, giving away items of her wedding outfit in the lobby was something else entirely.

"Why don't you come to my office while we sort this out?" Mareko suggested. He could fix this. He'd get one of the producers to track down the groom, the man could apologise for whatever real or imagined transgression was holding this woman back from holy matrimony with him, they'd push the wedding back an hour if they needed and then everything could proceed as planned.

*I hope the chefs haven't started cooking the fish yet.*

Paige looked at him closely. "You want me to marry him."

"Yes." Mareko answered honestly. There was no point lying.

"I won't." Her voice was strained, weaker than such a declaration should be and hope flared in his chest.

"Let's discuss this somewhere more private. Is there someone I can fetch for you while we wait? Your mother, perhaps?"

Her face went as white as the fabric of her dress under the heavy beading. "No," she croaked. "Definitely not my mother. She didn't approve of this as it was. To call it off now..." she shook her head. "She'll be so disappointed in me," she finished on a whisper Mareko wasn't sure he was supposed to hear. Then she squared her shoulders and met his eyes dead on, igniting a flame in his blood. "Thank you for your offer, but no. If I'm still at the resort, they'll find me and for once in my life I have no intention of being browbeaten into something to make others happy. I need to leave immediately."

"What about our place?" Rosa piped up beside Mareko. If he were honest with himself, he'd admit he'd almost forgotten she was there, but he looked down at her now, frowning.

"No, Rosa. Miss Beckett and I can meet in my office."

"So, you do know who I am." He looked back up into those green eyes which were sparkling with a wry humour, and offered a small shrug in return.

"There's only one reality show that's booked out my entire resort for a televised wedding, Miss Beckett."

"Doctor Beckett," she corrected. "And if the resort belongs to you, I wish you the best of luck in explaining my disappearance. Rachel," she called over his shoulder. "Would you be so kind as to call me a taxi?"

"Don't do it, Rachel," Mareko advised over his shoulder, feeling for the poor woman as she looked caught between the two of them hesitantly. "Look," he said to Paige in a quieter voice, "Rosa's idea isn't bad. We have a bungalow here, a little away from the guest houses. Why don't we take you there and you can calm down. Nobody from the production team will find you until you are ready, and we can sort this out?" The production team and all guests were booked to stay for another three nights. That gave Mareko plenty of time to convince her to follow through with the wedding. They'd have to place another food order with their supplier, but that cost would easily be offset by the success of the show and the business it would bring in.

Paige – Doctor Beckett – eyed him suspiciously. "I met you five minutes ago. What makes you think I'll agree to go to your house?"

Mareko smiled, the same one he'd often heard his staff

call his shark grin. "We will not ring a taxi for you today, Doctor Beckett. And unless I am very much mistaken, someone will be looking to escort you to your wedding minutes from now. We have a four-bedroom bungalow and you'll be with Rosa and my mother. I assure you," he said silkily, lowering his voice an octave and fighting against every stirring in his blood, "your virtue is under no threat from me, nor is your safety. After all, I intend to see you wed to another man as soon as possible."

# CHAPTER 2

*B*ungalow, Paige thought, was rather a misnomer. Sure, the structure looked much like the others she'd seen around the resort – crafted from dark wood native to the Pacific, topped with a thatched dome that stood high in the brilliant blue sky. But it was huge. Bigger than the resort's lobby itself. And where the rest of the resort lightened the heavy wooden beams with whitewashed furniture and licks of aqua paint, the partitions that separated rooms in this structure were painted a cheery yellow, clashing vibrantly with the overstuffed red sofas that took up most of the living space.

Rosa slipped past her into the house. "I'm going to get my sticker book to show you!"

Paige turned in time to see the hotel owner, Mareko Osa – he'd introduced himself while they hustled through the lush garden paths away from the main area of the resort – wrestling her suitcase up the steps of the wide porch.

"Would you like some help?" She made the offer instinctively, years of trying to please others bubbling up and spilling out before she could catch them and swallow them down again. He didn't deserve her help. He was still going to try and convince her to marry Patrick after all.

*Patrick.* Disappointment rang through her at the thought. Not at him. Her ex-fiancé was certainly a manipulative sonofabitch, but most of her regret turned inward. She should have seen it earlier. Perhaps if she hadn't been so lonely that she'd signed up for a reality show after a romcom binge and half a bottle of wine. The thought was sobering. Patrick had disappointed her, but was she really any better, disappointing all her family and the few friends that had gathered here for their nuptials?

She'd left a note, of course. Manners still mattered, even when leaving someone at the altar. Rachel would pass it along to whichever member of the production team went looking for her. It apologised for the situation, broke her engagement and informed them she had left Samoa. Maybe the last point wasn't quite truthful, but there was no way she was letting the production team think they could find her and talk her into walking down the aisle after all. Never mind her parents. God, they'd been horrified enough at her decision to go on the show in the first place, and aghast at the idea of a televised wedding. Adding runaway bride to the mix would be a tacky step too far.

Paige had been hoping to make them happy by finding love and settling down. Now that goal was further away than it had ever been.

Mareko hefted her suitcase inside the door and placed it to the side, carefully not meeting her eyes. "It's no trouble," he said, and Paige marvelled at the way the words sounded rolling off his tongue in that melodic accent. She'd noticed how attractive he was in the reception area of course, the same way one noticed that a sunset was pretty to look at, but now that her veil of panic and rage had lessened, she took a moment to study him and realised attractive had been an understatement. He was beautiful. Smooth brown skin, dark eyes with small lines that feathered out, the firm line of his nose and a strong jaw that betrayed not a hint of stubble. And those lips... full and sculpted, Michelangelo's David himself would have wept in envy.

Mareko cleared his throat, and she wrenched her eyes away, heat crawling up her cheeks.

*Shit.*

She'd been single a half hour, if that! Staring at another man's mouth was hardly appropriate, even if the bow of his upper lip could tempt a nun.

She must be delirious. Probably something to do with the two glasses of champagne she'd had after forgoing breakfast, or the fact that the control top underwear she was *still inexplicably wearing* prevented her from taking full breaths.

"I very much appreciate you letting me rest here until I can get a ride to the airport." She stressed the second half of the sentence and his eyes glinted in acknowledgement. "Would it be possible to change into something more comfortable?"

Mareko's eyes travelled over her dress, darkening as they did so, and Paige's limited breath hitched in her chest. She wasn't sure if it was knowing he still thought she should go ahead with the wedding or something else, but it was disconcerting. The moment lingered, pulsing in the air between them, something thick and unfamiliar uncurling in her chest as his gaze met hers.

He took a step towards her but paused as a clacking sound echoed up to the high ceilings. An older Samoan woman rounded one of the wall sections, leaning heavily on a walking stick. Shorter than Mareko and wide-hipped, her silver-streaked hair was in a tidy bun on top of her head. She looked up at the two of them, then her soft face broke into a glorious smile, and she pelted them with rapid-fire Samoan.

"Tina. Tina!" Mareko held out both hands as if to ward off an attack. He responded in his own language once she quietened, then with a glance at Paige, added in English, "This is my mother, Penina Osa. Tina, this is Doctor Beckett, a guest of the resort."

His mother spoke again, gesturing between them, and he shook his head.

"She thinks you should get married," a voice supplied helpfully by Paige's elbow, and she looked down to see Rosa there, holding a sticker book.

"That seems to be a popular opinion," Paige murmured dryly, and Rosa shook her head.

"Not to whoever you were meant to marry today. To my dad."

"We've just met!" Paige exclaimed, and the room fell silent. Mareko and his mother both peered at her with identical dark gazes, though one lifted a sardonic brow. *Arsehole.*

"We've just met," Paige repeated firmly, and Rosa translated for her grandmother who merely spat "Pah," and waved her free hand dismissively. Apparently this was of little concern.

"Perhaps," Mareko suggested lightly, "your attire indicates it's something you're interested in."

Paige narrowed her eyes at him. "Speaking of my attire, I requested a location to change?"

Several minutes later, most of which were spent wrestling her various pairs of underwear off, Paige slipped into a calf-length floral sundress and relief soaked her bones as she began the tedious work of unpinning her hair and swiping over her face with makeup remover wipes. Finally, feeling fresh and comfortable, she emerged from the spare bedroom Rosa had proudly escorted her to and met the Osa family on the red sofas. She sank into the plush seating, letting out a gentle moan as it cradled her. A hug in furniture form.

"Rachel called," Mareko said to her left, and she twisted her neck to look at him. He'd undone the top two buttons of his snowy white shirt and the tanned hollow at the base of his throat drew her eye. For a man of such obvious strength and standing, it seemed almost vulnerable. For one heady, hedonistic moment, she wondered what it would be like to lick it. Then shame rolled over her. Mareko was kind enough to let her hide out in his home with his family while she played hide-and-seek with a team of people whose jobs might well depend on her, and she'd managed to spend the majority of the time since they met ogling him.

*Bad Paige.*

"The production team is in hysterics, apparently. They threatened to break down the door to the bridal suite if we didn't give them a key to prove you weren't there. Your groom has retreated to his brother's villa and ordered a bottle of whisky. And the resort arranged for a glass-bottomed boat cruise for your parents this afternoon, now that they've been assured multiple times that you have in fact left the island."

Paige focused on her shell pink manicure. "Yes," she replied quietly, guilt stirring in her stomach. "That all sounds about right."

"How are you?" He asked the question suddenly, as though it had exploded out of his mouth without requisite permission. She risked a glance up at him, at the dark brows knit together over eyes that were studying her far too closely. Paige pasted a smile on her face, partly out of habit and partly to prevent him seeing the gaping wound Patrick's betrayal and the shattering of her own rose-coloured glasses had left in her chest.

"I'll be fine," she assured him. "I always am." She'd used the word fine so often today it had lost all meaning.

"Hmmm," he replied, but Rosa spoke first.

"You shouldn't be," she announced. "That was really horrid, the things he said."

Surprise flitted through Paige. "Horrid?" She cocked a brow in Mareko's direction.

"Her mother was French, but went to boarding school in England," he responded. "It slips in sometimes."

Paige turned back to Rosa. "I'm not sure what you heard–"

"I heard everything," Rosa interrupted stubbornly. She turned to her father. "He said he didn't want to marry her and he only picked her so the audience would like him. He was going to divorce her in two years." The little girl turned towards her grandmother and appeared to translate Paige's humiliation into Samoan as well. Mareko's mother gasped and made the sign of the cross.

*Cool, cool, cool. Can't have enough people knowing that.*

Mareko's brows weren't knotted anymore, they were almost at his hairline.

"Is that true?"

Paige smiled weakly. "I didn't realise she'd heard so much."

"Never underestimate the power of a nine-year-old eavesdropper. They're also insatiable tattletales." His voice lowered to a growl. "And to think, they were going to make a mockery of marriage in my resort."

Paige lifted one shoulder in resignation. "I'm sure money made through false intentions spends equally well."

"Perhaps," he replied darkly. "But it doesn't feel as good as the money you make through honest endeavours."

Before he could say anything else, his mother spoke, a melodic string of language that ended with her pointing towards the large clock that hung above the dining table in the open plan room.

"I have to go out for a bit," Mareko said, standing and helping his mother up. "Will you be alright here for a little while?"

"You're leaving?" Paige asked, standing too.

"My father," Mareko said, waving a hand towards a tall bookcase stacked with family pictures. "He's ill. He's in an aged care facility not far from here. I take my mother to visit for an hour a day. You should be alright if you don't go outside. Don't answer the door until we get back."

Paige nodded, fantasies of the nap she was going to take already dancing in front of her eyes.

"Papa, can I stay with Paige?" Rosa asked.

"Not today, Rosa. Go and get your shoes."

Rosa pouted and Paige farewelled her imaginary respite. "She can stay," she offered. "I'm happy to have her for company." After all, if it wasn't for Rosa, she might still be wedged into elastic corsetry, being toasted by a man who was simply using her for personal gain. As far as Paige was concerned, Rosa was a hero.

*Perhaps I'll by her a pony before I go back to New Zealand.*

"Fine," Mareko relented, and Rosa bounced lightly on her toes. "But you be good," he instructed Rosa.

"Always, Papa!" Her giggle drifted up to the rafters and Paige's own spirits lifted with it. "We'll be on our best behaviour!"

MAREKO COULD HEAR hysterical laughter from inside the bungalow before he set foot on the bottom step.

*This does not bode well.*

His visits with his father always left him feeling scraped raw, guilt and determination clawing at his insides in equal measure. The last thing he needed was to return to another scene of madness with the beautiful palagi girl in the middle of it all.

But when he stepped inside the bungalow, it was Rosa he saw, wearing the sparkling wedding gown, standing on the coffee table and performing what he recognised as her dance routine to 'Mamma Mia'.

He'd seen it a lot.

After a minute he realised he could hear it as well, blaring tinnily from the speakers of his old laptop, perched on the counter near Paige as she tried to mimic Rosa's movements.

"Step, step, arm?"

"Step, *arms*, step," Rosa corrected. "Let's take it from the top."

Mareko cleared his throat and the pair spun to face him.

"Hello," he offered.

"Papa, hi!" Rosa hitched the fall of fabric up to her armpits and leapt off the table onto skinny brown legs. "Look what Paige let me try on! Don't I look like a princess?"

"You look beautiful. Are you sure you should be wearing Doctor Beckett's wedding gown though? What if it gets dirty?"

A soft snort sounded from where Paige had flopped on the couch. "She could wear it into the ocean for all I care. I'm not going to have any use for it, am I?"

"Perhaps not," Mareko forced a lightness he didn't feel into his tone. "Never say never."

"I'm saying never to Patrick."

"You'll have to forgive me if your choice of soundtrack makes me doubt your commitment to spinsterhood."

Her eyes burned with emerald fire. "Your daughter chose the music."

"Ah," he exaggerated a wince. "Then you'll have to forgive her. Her mother's taste, obviously."

"Don't lie, Papa, you love it!" Rosa grabbed at his hand. "Dance with me."

Mareko spun her in a quick circle. "I cannot stay, afa'fine. I have to return to my office. There is much to be dealt with after the excitement of today."

"But it's almost dinnertime!"

"Your tinamatua will be here to eat with you shortly. She has gone to the spa for a massage for her bad leg, and they will drive her home in a golf cart when she is done."

"I want to eat with you."

"I know, Rosa. But it is not possible tonight." Mareko knelt in front of his daughter. The scent of peaches wafted up from the fabric of Paige's dress and the rush of desire that followed shocked him. He'd known her only a few hours, but he was already sure he'd never be able to smell peaches again without thinking of her blinking those jewel toned eyes up at him, the sun falling on her hair like a halo. Some things a man couldn't forget.

*And some things a man should.*

"Come on, Rosa," the woman in question said. "They've still got my credit card on file. Let's order the most expensive thing on the menu."

"I want pizza."

"Or pizza," Paige amended. "And we can get fruit cocktails in fancy glasses. How does that sound?"

Rosa eyed her, disappointment still tugging the corners of her mouth downward. "And you promise you'll learn the dance?"

"I promise I'll *try* to learn the dance," Paige clarified. "Dancing is not my area of expertise, but I'll do the very best I can."

"Okay." Rosa sniffed. "You can go then, Papa."

Mareko bent down to hug his daughter, shooting Paige a grateful look over her small, dark head. Their guest grinned in response and his chest tightened. Indigestion, no doubt.

"I'll walk your dad out, Rosa," she said. "Go into my suitcase and see if you can find my makeup bag. You can give me a makeover while we wait for our pizza."

Paige waited by the door while he shrugged his suit jacket back on. Despite the hint of dusk in the air, the tropical heat still packed a punch, but he'd be damned if anyone caught him in the office looking less than professional. The Moananui Resort had suffered enough through the unprofessional conduct of his predecessor. When he'd put himself to rights they stepped out onto the wide porch and she spoke.

"I'd like to thank you for speaking English when you can in front of me. It's a kind gesture and I appreciate it."

Mareko nodded tightly. "It's no trouble. I learnt English in school and lived internationally until two years ago. Rosa was born in Geneva, and her mother and I spoke English to each other as our primary language while she was growing up. I'm ashamed to admit that her English is probably superior to her Samoan at this stage." His chest tightened at the reminder. His parents had begged him to return to Samoa full time after Rosa's birth, but he'd been worried that living on Upolu full time would reveal the truth of his indifference for his wife.

Hélène had been an exceptional woman and a brilliant sommelier, but he had never been in love with her. In truth, their affair would have ended naturally had they not fallen pregnant with Rosa. If he hadn't been too ashamed to return, maybe he would have noticed the financial problems the resort was facing – the unpaid creditors and the expenses that rose directly in proportion to the number of luxury items the general manager seemed to be acquiring. Fighting back the wave of rage that rose every time he thought of the other man's deception, he returned his attention to Paige.

"You are very good with her," he admitted, and was relieved to see her smile, a star in the darkening sky.

"I love children," she admitted to him, a wistful look creeping into her eyes. "I was hoping to have some of my own in the future, but I suppose all of those plans will have to wait now."

Mareko cocked a brow. "You are sure you will not reconsider your marriage? Many men make mistakes in the leadup to a wedding, particularly one with such high stakes."

Paige glowered at him, and it was all Mareko could do not to snatch his words back out of the air and stuff them inside his mouth. He wanted that smile back, that softness in her green eyes like the lagoon on a calm day.

"I'm positive. He could come crawling on his knees brandishing the Hope Diamond and I'd be hard pushed not to kick him while he was down. I will compromise on a great many things in a relationship, Mr Osa, but a spouse who wants to be with me is not one of them."

Mareko blinked, hard. No. No, he couldn't ask her to do

that. Not when he had first-hand knowledge of how a loveless marriage felt, the cold blades of guilt and disinterest sliding under skin as spouses moved around each other like ambivalent satellites. Swallowing, he acknowledged her point with a tilt of his head. "I understand, and I won't ask again. Please forgive me for checking. Obviously, there will be significant negotiations between the resort and the production company over the fact that the event did not take place. It is essential that I understand the situation properly before entering into such discussions."

Paige hmmphed in response.

"What are your plans now?" The question that had been dogging him since he'd first escorted her along the palm-lined path to his fale in her wedding dress wrenched free and his chest pinched as he waited for her answer.

*Indigestion*. He rubbed at the spot with his fist. *Must have been the third espresso.*

"I don't know," she sighed, her eyes fixing on the beach that lay metres away from the path to his front porch, the sparkling sapphire swells lapping at the shore in a gentle lullaby. "I took a leave of absence from my job for the show and it included the honeymoon period. I'm not due to return for a month. Part of me relishes the idea of four weeks of freedom to do whatever I want without any busybodies poking their nose into my business, but my flatmate has already messaged to say there are paparazzi outside our house asking her about the cancelled wedding. I have enough savings to live on, but I'd prefer not to spend it all. If I'd gone through with it today, the show would have covered a honeymoon and Patrick and I would have moved in together soon after returning to New Zealand."

"Stay here."

Paige looked at him, eyes wide with surprise. Honestly,

the offer was a surprise to Mareko himself, but the more he turned the idea over in his mind, the more sense it made.

"Rosa is on school holidays, and as you may have noticed, my mother is getting too old to watch her properly during the day. She needs a nanny, someone to look after her while I work to keep her stimulated and entertained. We have a spare room, and Rosa likes you."

"But the guests, the production team. . ."

Mareko waved a dismissive hand. "They leave two days from now. You can stay here at the bungalow until the coast is clear and then the resort is yours. I'll organise a car you can use to travel around the island. You have a driver's licence, yes?"

"Yes," Paige answered faintly.

"You can swim? I assume your first aid skills are up to date."

"They are. I can swim; I'm a great swimmer, actually."

"Perfect." Mareko shrugged. "I can't think of anyone more qualified to watch Rosa. If you're open to the idea, we would be lucky to have you as a nanny."

*And it will leave me free to work out a solution to the situation you've left the resort in.*

Paige opened her mouth, but before she could speak, Rosa bounded out the front door, still sheathed in Art Deco-inspired couture, with red lipstick smeared across her face like a tiny, well-dressed version of The Joker.

"What are you doing out here? It's taking *forever*."

Mareko smiled down at his daughter's exasperation, so like his own impatience when he was a child.

"We are discussing Doctor Beckett's job prospects. Would you like her to be your nanny while you're on holidays?"

"Oh, *yes*," Rosa breathed reverentially. "We'll have time

to learn so many dances." She peered up at Paige. "Wait until you see my routine for 'Moves Like Jagger.'"

"An inspired choice," Paige murmured, giving Mareko a 'what-the-hell' look. He hid a smirk. "I look forward to seeing it."

"It's settled then," Mareko nodded. "I'll get the paperwork drawn up so you can receive wages. Welcome to The Moananui Resort staff, Doctor Beckett. It will be a pleasure having you."

# CHAPTER 3

The stress of being Paige Beckett's employer was going to kill him.

Mareko sat in his dark office in the dull blue glow of his computer screen one week after hiring Paige, and cursed the Him of Poor Choices Past for making the offer at all.

He wasn't a fool. He knew he was avoiding returning home. He even knew why. It didn't make it sting less.

He was infatuated. For seven nights now he'd returned home to a scene of utter domestic bliss, the kind he'd always envisioned growing up - the bungalow glowing gold as day turned to dusk, calling to him like a moth to flame. It beckoned him with the low thump of music that reached out and wrapped itself like a fist in his innards, pulling him forward and up the wide porch steps each night to find Paige dressed in a flowing summer dress dancing with Rosa, or the two of them playing cards, or painting, her hair like spun silver and her eyes like jewels as they looked up to greet him.

It was intolerable. He'd never been so aroused by the idea of simple domesticity. Perhaps because his late wife

Hélène had never given herself so fully to the domestic role. He'd thought it was simply her nature – a modern woman, passionate about her work as a sommelier. But later she'd revealed that she'd never enjoyed motherhood, never enjoyed being married to *him*. He'd stood in the living room of their Egyptian apartment as she told him she was leaving them – little Rosa a mere six years old – every plant and photo on their shelves suddenly feeling like props in a pantomime of his life he hadn't known was being performed.

Worst of all had been the relief. It had flooded him even as he and Hélène had shouted their final words into the crumbling void of their life together. Relief that he no longer had to *pretend*, that the shame over not loving her back was somehow justified by her own lack of desire for him. Had it not been for her rejection of Rosa — a secret he would keep from his daughter until death – and the fatal outcome of that night, they could have divorced amicably. He could have returned to Samoa with his daughter without the cloud of grief and guilt that had haunted their homecoming.

Returning to the bungalow at night now that Paige was there... It felt like coming home in a different way. A settled golden warmth, the kind that soaked into his bones and revived him after hours staring at a screen. It was a potent reminder of his own childhood, when he and his parents worked themselves to the point of exhaustion running the resort in the early days before they could afford a full staff, but each night they would gather around the table by candlelight to pray and eat together, his father's booming laugh wrapping around him like an embrace while he slurped down his mother's palusami.

The food must be part of it, he decided. Since Rosa had

been in Paige's care during the days, Penina's love of cooking seemed to have been rekindled. He was returning less and less to meals delivered from the resort kitchen for supper and more to some of his childhood recipes steaming hot on the table. His mother was sleeping later and had more energy. He'd even been mildly traumatised after returning from the bathroom during one of their daily visits to his father's care home to find them locked in an amorous embrace, springing apart like jack-in-the-boxes when he cleared his throat.

Mareko could appreciate their love in theory of course, but to come across it in person was something else altogether. The drive back to the resort had been one of the most awkward of his life.

Sighing, he pushed back from his desk and reached for his suit jacket, shrugging it on for the walk across the resort. His fears were confirmed when he reached the bungalow to find Paige sitting cross-legged on the floor, draped in a simple cotton dress that skimmed the lush bounty of her curves while Rosa French-braided her hair.

"Papa!" Rosa abandoned her hairdressing and flung herself across the wooden floorboards to wrap herself around him. "You're home early!"

In truth it was after eight, but Mareko's avoidance techniques along with the production company negotiations had stretched far into the night this week.

"Malo, afa'fine." He bent down to press a kiss against his daughter's glossy hair. "'O a mai 'oe?" *How are you?*

"Manuia, fa'afetai."

"Good," he smiled down at her. "And you, Paige? How are you?"

"Manuia, fa'afetai," she responded sunnily, and he

hitched a brow at her flawless pronunciation at the positive response.

"Rosa has been working with me on a little of the language," his nanny smiled. "I hope you don't mind, but there are Post-Its all over the place with translations on them now."

"Paige is going to learn Samoan and live here forever," Rosa announced.

"Don't threaten me with a good time, honey," Paige warned. "It sounds like fun and games now, but when you're sixteen the idea of having a nanny still watching over you will be social Guantanamo."

Mareko snorted at her description. "Were you a hellion at sixteen?" Lord knows, he'd have loved to have been, but there had never been time after helping his parents with the resort. There wasn't a job in the business he hadn't undertaken growing up - even now he was sure he could still clean a bathroom in under ninety seconds.

"Not a chance," Paige replied, sifting her fingers through the silvery-gold strands of hair Rosa had left untethered. "I was studying every night until at least eleven and volunteering on the weekends. The only thing even slightly rebellious I've ever done is try to find love outside of the walls of the local pub, and look how that turned out." She spread her arms wide. "I was the dictionary definition of a nerd. Speaking of, I have a few things I'd like to go over with you later this evening, if you have time?"

"Of course."

Awareness hummed through his blood as he and Rosa set the table, all through dinner and Rosa's bedtime routine. The sheer force of will it took not to rest a hand at the nape of Paige's neck or inhale her peach scent as they brushed by each other had his nerves tight and drained by the time his daughter drifted off to sleep.

*I could use a drink*. He was dialling room service before the thought had left his head. Ordering a single cup of 'ava for himself sat uneasy given the usual ceremony associated with the beverage, but he longed for the relaxing effect of the drink to soothe away the rough edge of tension that twined around his limbs every time he caught a glimpse of his nanny.

"Do you want a drink?" He directed the question at Paige even as the line rang.

"Ooh, yes please." Her face lit up at the possibility.

*Right. She's supposed to be on her honeymoon*. A woman like Paige, always careful and prepared, would likely have studied the resort's menus before arriving, yet he hadn't seen her with a single alcoholic beverage yet. Not even in the wake of her ex-fiancé's betrayal.

"What would you like?"

"I don't mind. You choose." A shadow passed across her face. "Nothing with rum," she intoned darkly.

He ordered her a coconut margarita and she looked delighted with it when it arrived, plucking the pink paper umbrella from the rim to tuck behind her ear. They took their drinks out to the porch, settling side by side at the wide table, the wood still warm from the sun's rays. Above the palm trees that swayed between his fale and the ocean the sky was painted in vivid streaks of orange and pink, sliding into indigo as the night crept upward from the horizon.

Mareko sipped the 'ava, tilting his head back to let the liquid trickle down his throat, closing his eyes and breathing deeply as warmth suffused his body, a reassuring weight settling into his bones in the wake of the familiar taste. Paige, he saw opening his eyes, was far more enthusiastic with her approach - half of her drink was already gone and she was doing a happy little dance in her seat as she licked salt from the rim of her glass. The sight of her sweet, pink tongue dancing out to capture crystalline flecks and the hum of satisfaction that followed on the balmy air almost undid him. He groaned, and her eyes flicked up to meet his.

"Sorry, was that strange?"

"Not at all," Mareko croaked. "Perfectly normal."

*So normal I probably need to adjust myself.*

Paige stared at him as if she could read his thoughts, and Mareko fumbled to loosen his tie as his throat constricted.

"I wanted to talk about the programme for Rosa's summer holidays," Paige announced, setting her drink down and pulling out a folder from Lord knows where. "I've compiled a schedule that I believe covers everything, but I'd love it if you could take a look and offer any feedback." She passed it across the table and he took it, the heft sending a spark of surprise through him. The spark spread into a fully-fledged flame of concern as he opened it and perused the contents. As a business owner, her efficiency impressed him. As a parent, the obvious effort did too. But as a man? Where was the fluidity? The freedom? He'd given her the job more as a favour than anything, and she'd come to him with a strategy that could be used to write educational policy.

*This woman does not know how to relax.*

"What do you think?" Paige asked, and he looked up to see her watching him carefully, eyes large and worried behind the salted rim of her glass.

"It's very well-prepared," he replied slowly. "But you've made a grave error."

PANIC SLICED like a scalpel blade through the spell the evening's magic had wound around Paige, leaving her cold.

*An error?* She racked her brain, searching for something she'd overlooked. She'd used the Samoan national curriculum for guidance, and supplemented it with the New Zealand one for good measure. Outings were planned for locations of cultural significance, for spiritual acknowledgement and to commune with nature. There was an hour a day set aside for developing life skills - financial literacy, nutrition, and cooking, cybersafety and first aid, as well as dedicated periods of time for dancing and online self-defence tutorials.

"I-I'm sorry," Paige stammered, squeezing the apology past the tightness in her throat. Her heart pounded a staccato rhythm in her chest and she raised her voice to drown out the erratic thumping. "I didn't think I'd missed anything. If you give me a chance to make it right—" she shook her head, frustration lighting a white-hot path down her spine "—I can do better. I *will* do better."

*I will* be *better.*

Silence answered her. From far away the delicate trill of a bird echoed around the edges of the porch where the atmosphere had thickened, weighed down by her failure. When she couldn't stand it anymore, Paige dared a look at Mareko. He was watching her through the full sweep of his dark lashes, his gaze fierce. Beneath the shadow of stubble, a muscle jumped in his firm jaw as he studied her. Paige dropped her gaze away from his face, watching the play of muscles in his hand as long fingers gripped the half coconut shell that he'd been drinking from.

"What the hell was that?" His voice was low, dangerous.

"What was what?" She didn't have nearly enough pluck to pull off the flippancy she was aiming for. Her voice wavered like a ukulele string out of tune.

"What just happened? Where did you go?"

"I'm right here."

"Oh, no. No, no, no." Out of the corner of her eye, Paige saw Mareko gesture at her with his coconut. "That woman wasn't the Paige Beckett I know. *That* woman almost melted into a shaking heap of nerves on my porch when I said she'd made a mistake."

Paige grimaced, discomfort pricking at the base of her skull. "I have a thing about mistakes."

"We all make them."

"I don't."

"With all due respect," Mareko's voice held a sardonic twist, "the very reason you're staying in my guest room begs to differ."

"That's different." It wasn't, but one internal crisis at a time. "I don't make mistakes with work. Usually." Paige hastened to add. "Sometimes there might be a problem I need to consult on, or I might struggle with a particular patient, but that stuff —" she nodded towards the folder "— the paperwork, the research, that's my skill set. I don't like to find out I haven't lived up to expectations in that area."

"Whose expectations?"

Paige's head shot up. "Pardon?"

"I said, whose expectations are you not living up to?"

Nausea rose in her throat, and she swallowed it down. "Mine."

"Hmmm." He knew she wasn't being entirely truthful. It was there in the slight downward turn of his lips. "Perhaps you are being a little hard on yourself."

*You have no idea.*

"Perhaps so. But a woman in my position needs to be hard on herself. God knows, everyone else will be."

Dark eyes searched her face, and she looked down, thumbing away a bead of condensation that trickled down the side of her glass and hoping the cool drop would work to reduce the heat climbing her cheeks. There was nothing unkind in his gaze, but the uncomfortable sensation of being studied too closely pricked the back of her neck.

"I mean," she continued, forcing a lightness she didn't feel into her tone, "the comments alone from the reality show would have crushed a lesser woman."

"But not you?" His voice was silky, soft. A trap to be sure, but she couldn't help leaning in a little more.

"I'm used to being watched closely." At his quizzical look, she shrugged. "I'm an IVF baby. My parents wanted a large family, but they ended up with just me. There's often a certain level of focus on only children. I'm sure a lot of their anxiety came from the fact that they worked so hard to have me. But it did mean that there was a bit of pressure to be enough – a worthy return on their investment, if you will."

"I will not."

"Pardon?"

"That's a terrible way to think of yourself," Mareko ground out. "For any child."

Paige turned that over in her head. "Do you have siblings Mareko?"

"No," he shook his head. "But I barely got to be a child at all." He gestured around himself. "My grandfather broke ground on The Moananui, a few beachfront fale and an umu. Eighty percent of Samoa is held under customary land law – it is owned by the families and passed down. My father inherited it from his father and I from him. My whole life before I left Samoa to study was this land, and the buildings on it. We worked constantly – early mornings, late nights. Whenever I wasn't in school or church, I was working here at the resort. Buildings were added, the facilities modernised and Westernised, we slowly added staff, but there isn't a role in this resort I don't have firsthand experience of. My parents had high expectations of me certainly, but that's because they worked so hard themselves." He pinned Paige with his eyes. "Businesses are an investment, Paige. They have downturns, lean years, spurts of growth and profit. That is the nature of it. People?" He shook his head. "People are not investments. *Children* are not investments. They are not something to be celebrated in the good times and ignored in the bad. The only person who decides the worth of a human is the individual themselves."

"It's a lovely idea." Paige twisted her mouth into a smile. "But I believe you just said I've made a grave error in the paperwork, so you'll have to forgive me when I've clearly provided you with a downturn."

Mareko tossed her folder on the table. "The mistake is not in the paperwork, Paige. The paperwork *is* the mistake."

Paige stared at him, flummoxed. "I don't understand."

"Your schedule is beyond fault for homeschooling," Mareko shrugged. "But it is the holidays. Rosa, she needs freedom. She needs fun. These skills you've outlined, they are wonderful things to have, but she needs to have a childhood first. I didn't, and it's the one thing I have sworn I will give Rosa, no matter the cost." He reached over and laid his hand on top of hers. Warmth suffused her, a tingling sensation that raced up her arm and pulsed through her chest. She stared at their hands, the bronze of his skin against the cream of hers. They looked like art. And the way his skin settled against her, gentle and firm, like she was precious. Porcelain. She *felt* like art in that moment. Like something beautiful, bigger than herself here at this moment. Her heart skipped a beat, then two.

Mareko continued, seemingly unaffected. "Rosa adores you, Paige. She's made that clear. She loves having someone who can keep up with her, who can match her enthusiasm. Someone who is willing to dance to silly songs and play dress ups and practice dolphin dives in the resort pool with her. Those activities are all the education she needs at this point in the year. By all means, take her on hikes, cook with her, teach her first aid. But please do those things because you will both enjoy them, not out of some obligation to prove you are worthy of this job."

Paige deflated like a balloon, her desire evaporating as disappointment rushed in to fill the void his words left in her.

"I'm sorry." *How did I get it so wrong?*

"Don't be sorry." Mareko's hand tightened on hers, warm and solid, reassuring her. "Spending time with you is enough for her." His thumb skimmed the skin at the back of her hand, back and forth, electricity lighting the nerve endings he brushed like a pendulum. "*You* are enough."

The desire was back. It was almost too much - the tropical breeze, the vibrant sunset, and the beautiful man holding her hand and telling her everything she'd longed to hear. She closed her eyes and let the moment soak soul-deep into her, the usually-jagged edges of her mind smoothed by the tranquillity of the island.

*And the tequila. Can't disregard the tequila.*

"You've been so kind," she said, turning her hand under his and interlacing their fingers. "I don't quite know what I would have done without you that day."

Mareko chuckled, but it sounded strained and the

dreamy sensation enveloping her sharpened into a point, tunnelling down below her belly button to the space between her legs. "I have no doubt that you would have been fine, Paige."

"Perhaps." She opened her eyes to find him staring at her mouth. "But perhaps being fine isn't enough for me now. Maybe," she continued, her voice barely more than a whisper, "I want more."

He lifted his eyes to hers and she swallowed at the richness of his dark pupils lit with desire. Her nerves were back, but not the swirling maelstrom that had tossed her out of her scripted life and into Mareko's on her wedding day. These nerves were like honey, sticky and rich, spreading out from her abdomen, coating her in liquid armour formed of bravery and abandon.

"Paige—" Mareko began, but she lifted one hand to his stubble-roughened cheek and he fell silent.

"I think," she said slowly, "we can do better than fine."

Then she leaned in and kissed him.

# CHAPTER 4

Gods help him, she tasted like coconut, salt and sin. Sweet. Tangy.

*Forbidden.*

Desire flared in Mareko's blood, twisting and spreading like a forest fire until every inch of him was consumed by lust. He pulled her chair closer and opened his mouth, deepening the kiss. Her gasp was like music to his ears, his own pulse keeping the rapid staccato of island drums as she sifted the fingers of her free hand through his hair. Mareko shivered, angling his head to capture Paige's lips again and again, sipping at her mouth.

*Lagi. Heaven.*

He should know better than to blaspheme, but right now this was the closest he could imagine getting to the pearly gates. He cupped Paige's face in his hands, her skin like silk, warm and soft. He'd thought holding her hand was magic, but it had nothing on the way she felt in his arms, her lips pressed against his.

Changing the angle of the kiss, he ran his tongue across the seam of her lips and to his everlasting gratitude she opened underneath him, welcoming him, the sweet tangle of their tongues taking the kiss from simply heavenly to sublime.

He'd been at half-mast since he'd watched her lick the salt of the rim of her glass, and now his cock flared to life in response to the feel of her in his arms, her lips on his. He was on the edge of something —

"Mareko," she moaned in between kisses, and the sound of his name was enough to bring him to his senses as soundly as if he'd been doused with a bucket of cold water. The sharp glitter that had been swirling in his chest faded, leaving a hollow that echoed his name.

He pulled back, disentangling their hands. Paige made as if to move towards him again, and he held up a hand to stop her. The effort was painful, his erection straining against the seam of his pants as he took her in, plush pink lips swollen, green eyes huge in her heart shaped face, the subtle jut of her nipples under the thin cotton of her dress. She was a vision.

*She's an employee.*

He'd done a lot of things in his life that he regretted. But in that moment, under the starry light of the Southern Cross, Mareko hated himself.

Everything he'd worked for since he'd returned to Samoa, everything his aiga had worked for their whole lives – he'd risked it all in one act of complete unprofessionalism. His stomach churned as he ran through the possibilities. Lawsuits, accusations of sexual harassment, even an unfounded rumour amongst staff would cause irreparable damage. After everything the resort had already suffered... Not to mention what would happen to Paige's reputation if they became involved.

"This was a mistake."

Paige recoiled back into her seat as if he'd brandished a weapon. "Oh."

"We should not have – *I* should not have kissed you. It was extremely unprofessional."

"I kissed you," she pointed out quietly, her eyes back on her cocktail glass.

"And I kissed you back. It wasn't appropriate. You have my sincere apologies."

"Okay?" She said it like it was a question, but there could be no questioning the fallout that would come from this lapse in his professionalism if it became resort knowledge. The Moananui Resort had worked hard to retain staff in the wake of Edwin Glass's betrayal. Employees would drop like flies – highly judgemental flies – if word got out that Mareko was using his position as the general manager to seduce employees. He couldn't do it – couldn't risk his family's future for a mere flare of lust, even if the flame licked hotter at him than anything he'd ever experienced.

"It's not personal," he assured her, yearning to wash away the hurt that was written all over her face.

She laughed bitterly.

"It feels pretty personal to me. Don't worry, though, Mr Osa." She drained the last of her drink, the tinkling of ice in the glass a poor soundtrack to the film of discomfort that had settled over the table. "I won't make such a foolish mistake again."

"Mareko, please," he murmured, her formal language like a burr against his skin, already stretched too tight with shame and with – dammit – wanting her still.

She merely looked at him, her eyes dark in the porch shadows. The urge to comfort her, reassure her, rose like a well inside him.

"Perhaps we could simply chalk this up to the drinks,"

he suggested. Her pert nose wrinkled, but he hurried onward. "I'm sure you still have some unresolved feelings regarding your recent relationship. The night, the liquor." He gestured expansively, taking in the inky sky, the candles made with a special essence to keep bugs away, "It's no surprise we made an error in judgement."

Paige stood gracefully, her glass clasped firmly in her hand.

"My fiancé did not love me," she said clearly, her voice like a bell in the still evening. "Everything he said to me was a lie, a deception created to promote himself and his interests. As soon as I learned that, any feelings I had for him were gone. How could I feel anything for someone I never truly knew? You are right about one thing, though." She pinned him with her gaze. "I have made a terrible error in judgement."

Before he could speak, she left, the riotous colour of her skirt whirling around her legs as she strode inside, faster than he'd seen her move since her wedding day.

Mareko sat back in his chair heavily, the still, warm air suddenly oppressive. He reached for his 'ava and gulped it down, but it failed to soothe him.

*What were you thinking?* His inner voice chided him and he shook his head, frustration prickling at his skin.

Madness, it was the only explanation. No matter how attractive Mareko had found women in the past, he had never been tempted to risk any part of his own life, or Rosa's future. Not since Hélène's betrayal. But something about Paige Beckett had inspired him to throw caution to the wind and risk it *all*. Everything he had. Rosa's entire legacy.

*It must be madness.*

Well, he was not a man to crumble at the first sign of madness. He would shore up his defences instead. Embrace routine. Limited interactions with a certain blonde temptress. A renewed focus on the resort's success. No more alcohol. He glared darkly at the now-empty coconut shell he'd been drinking from. Resisting a woman was no different than resisting liquor. All it took was a little determination. And Mareko Osa was the most determined man in the South Pacific.

PAIGE WOKE the next morning determined to start over. She'd tossed and turned the night before, sheets tangling around her legs as she replayed the scene on the porch. The candlelight. The drinks. Mareko's kind words. And the kiss… *holy crap, that kiss.*

Paige might not have spent her university days like her flatmates, hanging from the lips of every wanky philosophy student they could meet at bars with two dollar shots, but she had enough experience to know that the kiss she had shared with Mareko was nothing short of spectacular. If any of her previous romantic partners had kissed her like that, she'd never have unlocked lips long enough to get her doctorate.

Swinging her legs over the side of her borrowed bed, Paige stood by the window of Mareko's guest room and stretched. The tension that had coiled inside her since Mareko's rejection the night before dulled as she reached high into the air before bending to touch her tiptoes. Several more repetitions of the cycle and it had almost disappeared completely.

*There now*, she thought with almost vicious satisfaction. *Rejection is nothing that can't be cured with a little exercise and sunshine.*

A small voice whispered inside her that she'd know that more than most, but Paige ignored it. Listening to her critical inner voice had almost got her married to Patrick, after all.

Speaking of which, it had been over a week. It was probably past time for her to check in with the real world. Listening carefully for any sound of life in the bungalow, she crept out to the main living area. Rosa and Penina's doors were closed, but Mareko's was wide open, revealing a neatly made bed. There was no sign of the man himself though. He must already be at work.

*Guess he had no problems sleeping last night.*

Flicking the coffeemaker to life, she switched on her phone for the first time since her ill-fated wedding day and immediately muted it as a stream of notifications lit up the screen like a strobe light. Nothing like publicly abandoning your nationally-beloved fiancé at the altar to make a girl feel popular. Cradling her mug of coffee to her chest, she sank onto one of the red couches and began the tedious process of deleting almost every single message.

There were the ones from her flatmate Lily, letting her know that paparazzi were still loitering outside their shared residence. Ones from the few work friends she'd invited to the wedding, their first missives of concern as the wedding had been cancelled, then morphing into frustration and ending with photos of them paddleboarding and snorkelling. Her voicemail was full of requests for interviews and Paige dreaded to think how reporters had found her cell phone number. She'd have to change it when she returned to New Zealand, but for now she simply blocked every unfamiliar number.

Her mother had called too, thirty-three times. She hadn't left a message though, simply screeds of her name in red on

Paige's call log screen, wrenching Paige's chest tighter simply by virtue of existing. She typed out a quick message, assuring her mother of her wellbeing. It wouldn't be enough for Kathleen and Gregory Beckett – not after all the worry they'd suffered on her behalf growing up with her health issues, but it assuaged some of Paige's guilt. She'd left them a separate note with Rachel on her wedding day as well, but it was no surprise that her phone had blown up with them seeking explanations in the wake of her disappearance. Paige's breath grew shorter, sharper, at the idea of speaking to them in person, in hearing the disappointment in their voices.

No, messages were all she could manage right now.

It took her half an hour to clear the backlog before she even made it to her email.

Her inbox was a welcome relief - one hundred and eighteen new messages, but compared to her phone messages, which for the most part smacked of the voyeuristic desire to secure gossip, her emails were the usual mix of work, updates on her virtual book club and adverts from the meal subscription box she usually relied on. There were three exceptions, all from the same person.

Natalia Brunson.

Steeling herself, Paige opened the first one, then the next, and the next. Natalia's already-thin veneer of politeness evaporated from one email to the next, devolving into rants against Paige's character and threats of litigation. She claimed Paige had breached the filming contract by not going through with the ceremony, which was news to Paige. She'd studied the legal paperwork thoroughly, as had her independent counsel. Paige saved the emails to a separate folder so she wouldn't have to see them and set her phone aside.

Her coffee was cold now, and she placed the mug on the worn wooden floorboards beside the couch, lying back and staring up at the fan as it whirr-whirr-whirred above her head.

She didn't know how long she lay like that, letting the island warmth soak into her bones, staring at nothing. It had been too long since she'd let herself be. Before Patrick, definitely. Before her masters, probably. A vision came to her - she and her uni flatmates from her undergraduate years sprawled across beanbags in their draughty sharehouse, hungover and surrounded by fast food bags while a romantic comedy played on the TV.

Rosa crawled out of her bedroom at one point, lying on the floor next to the couch and staring upwards as well.

"What are we looking at?" Paige's charge whispered eventually.

"Nothing," Paige whispered back. "We're just thinking."

"Awesome."

It *was* awesome, Paige decided. After years of busting her arse trying to make everyone else happy, she was here, on a tropical island. She wasn't without responsibilities – she still had to be a nanny after all – but the pressure that had been sitting on her chest for the best part of a decade was lessening with every day that passed in Samoa.

Recalling Mareko's comments about her job from last night, she turned to Rosa.

"What do you want to do today?"

"Swimming," Rosa's response was decisive.

"Cool. Do you know CPR?"

"No."

"I can teach you after our swim if you want. It's an important skill to have near water."

Rosa nodded. "Then maybe one day I can be a doctor too. Or a dancer. Or a librarian."

Paige grinned at the openness and excitement in the younger girl's face. She remembered that feeling, the endless possibilities that lay out in front of kids who had no concepts of mortgages or night shifts. She'd wanted to be a jockey when she was Rosa's age, but by the age of fourteen she'd been five foot five with an arse for days, and her parents' hints about pursuing medicine had been more overt. "You can be all of those things. You can be anything you want, Rosa."

Penina shuffled out soon after and Paige started on omelettes for everyone, despite Rosa's assurances that they could just call the resort's kitchen and have some sent over. After that statement, Rosa finished the omelettes, while Paige and Penina supervised.

They spent the morning in the pool, swimming laps and practicing handstands, and Paige was thankful the last of the wedding guests had left several days ago so she could concentrate properly rather than jumping behind one of the decorative rocks that lined the pool's perimeter every time a new person approached. Rachel, the concierge, had been kind enough to inform her when the last people had checked out from the block of rooms reserved for guests and production staff, as well as when Patrick specifically had left. Idly, Paige wondered how much Mareko was paying the woman. It couldn't be enough. Her customer service skills were unparalleled.

After their swim, Paige ran Rosa through the basics of CPR, focusing on the techniques used for smaller children and infants – Rosa's thin arms would be next to useless in exerting enough pressure to revive an adult – but the girl took to it gamely, concentration etched into her face as she practised on a rolled-up towel under the shade of a poolside beach umbrella.

Their next few days followed the same pattern – Paige followed Rosa's lead in terms of interests for the day, attempting to slip in a few life skills along the way. They borrowed one of the resort's vans and drove up to To Sua Trench, one of the country's most photographed spots, where they explored the gardens, identifying different plants before descending the steep ladder and sitting on the small jetty to dip their feet in the turquoise water of the natural pool. They wandered through the markets, held in large open-air warehouses or constructed out of rough-hewn wooden beams while sheets of corrugated iron offered protection from the powerful island sun. Rosa chatted away happily to locals while Paige browsed long, cylindrical, hand-carved drums, flax-woven fans, sweeping skirts in bright colours, and jewellery made from shell and bone. She practised her conversational Samoan with stallholders and paid full price to the children who roamed the market lanes with trays of drinks and snacks around their necks without haggling, which disgusted Rosa.

"They're charging resort prices for something we could get at the supermarket!" Rosa hissed as Paige handed her a bottle of water covered in beads of condensation.

"But we're not at the supermarket," Paige pointed out, opening her own bottle and lifting it to her lips. Bliss. Despite the shadow of the market roof, the heat was still bordering on oppressive due to the day's lack of wind. Not even a light breeze shuffled the patterned tapa cloths that lay out for display at the stall they stood in front of. "Besides, you need to drink more water," she told Rosa. "I don't care how much papaya you put in your smoothies, it's still not as healthy for you as actual water."

In the afternoons, Mareko collected Rosa and Penina to visit with his father. It was practically the only time Paige saw him. He was gone in the mornings when she woke, and she retired to her room when he returned to the bungalow in the evenings. Where their interactions had been easy before her misguided attempt to kiss him, they were now stilted, the air growing thicker in her lungs every time she caught a glimpse of his dark hair or strong jaw out of the corner of her eye.

Part of it was the dynamics, she mused. Rejection was never a pleasant experience, but the added element of sharing a residence made it particularly tiresome. The memories of their night on the porch lingered like a bad smell, coating her with its stench. She wanted him, that was undeniable. And yet he'd rejected her, even going so far as to suggest her behaviour was the result of intoxication. Embarrassment flooded her every time she remembered the way he'd gently dislodged her from his embrace – hence her tendency to head to her room when Mareko was home. It was his house, after all. He'd been kind enough to offer her a job and a place to stay, and polite enough to try and excuse her clearly unrequited lust. The least she could do was give him space with his family without an awkward, infatuated interloper intruding.

Because there was no doubt about it. When it came to Mareko Osa, Paige was still deeply infatuated.

# CHAPTER 5

"*B*oss?" There was a knock on Mareko's door and he looked up to see Rachel standing there. "You wanted to see me?"

"Ah, yes." Mareko stood and gestured to the chairs in front of his desk. "Please, take a seat."

His concierge sank down into one of the aqua linen chairs. Like most of the hotel, Mareko's office floor was constructed of large white tiles, all the better to beat the Samoan heat. Plain white walls surrounded him on three sides, with a floor-to-ceiling window running the length of the office on the other, affording him a view of the lush gardens brimming with pink and yellow hibiscus flowers. Beyond the gardens, which doubled as a serene break space for staff, the hotel pool shimmered through the leaves, glinting wickedly in the sun as though to tempt him.

A foolish notion. Mareko Osa was not a man who was easily tempted.

"I understand that you've been managing the resort's marketing and social media for the last year," he said to Rachel, who nodded warily.

"Yes. Mr Glass assigned me the role on top of my concierge duties."

Of course Edwin had. More time for him to fritter away their profits by lining his own pockets.

"Did he increase your salary to compensate for the additional work?"

"He did not." The downward turn of Rachel's mouth indicated what she thought of that. Privately, Mareko agreed.

"I'll be relieving you of those duties from today," he informed Rachel. "Your pay will not be affected, but I will be speaking to the finance department about a bonus for the work you've done."

"Thank you, Mareko. I appreciate it."

Mareko nodded, pleased with himself, before noticing Rachel worrying her lip with her teeth. They'd gone to school together, he and Rachel. Every year since they were five, up through to finishing in the same class at seventeen. They hadn't been friends, though she might be the closest thing he had to one now – her daughter and Rosa often played together in the resort pool after school – but he knew her well enough to recognise what that gesture meant.

Leaning back in his leather chair, he crossed his arms over his chest. "What is it?"

To Rachel's credit, she didn't feign ignorance. "I don't want the job, Mareko. But I don't know that you should be taking on any additional responsibilities either." She swept a dark hand around his office. "You're in here before I arrive at six in the morning. You're in here when the bar staff leave at ten at night. Esafi from maintenance says you use the gym at five o'clock every morning, and your workload?" She blew out a breath and raised her eyebrows at the copious amounts of paper shuffled into semi-tidy stacks on his dark wooden desk. "It's the stuff of nightmares," she continued. "I worry about your health." She looked him dead in the eyes. "I worry about Rosa."

That did it. Mareko narrowed his eyes at his concierge. "Rosa is fine. She's fantastic."

"She's an amazing kid," Rachel replied evenly, not breaking eye contact. "But she's lonely. Having Doctor Beckett here has been excellent for her, but that is not a long-term solution. We need more managerial staff so that you can delegate some of your workload."

He had to give it to her, she had brass totoga. That, plus their shared history, drove him into honesty.

"There's no money. Edwin Glass ruined the resort economically. The finance department knows, obviously, but we tried to keep it quiet to avoid panic." He sighed. "The *One True Love* wedding would have restored us to the pre-Glass days and the additional publicity would have made us one of the most successful resorts in the South Pacific. But obviously that didn't happen." Mareko rapped his knuckles against a stack of staff feedback forms. "Until another reality show wants to promote us all over the Pacific, I'm it. I'm hiring. I'm firing. I'm doing marketing and event planning and statistical analysis, and I'll be back behind the bar making smoothies if I have to in order to dig us out from this hole."

"I suspected," Rachel said quietly. "Mr Glass's spending seemed...frivolous."

Mareko arched an eyebrow in acknowledgement. "I'm sorry if I'm not living up to your parenting standards right now, Rachel, but I'm trying to keep Rosa's legacy from crumbling into dust."

She nodded slowly. "I apologise for overstepping."

"You didn't," Mareko assured her. "And to be honest, I'm

glad Rosa has someone else looking out for her. Now come write a list of all our social media accounts and their log-ins so I can do an audit of where we stand with the different platforms."

Rachel left several minutes later and Mareko spent the next hour going through different sites, checking the log-in information she'd provided, accepting friend requests from the world over and clicking on the latest posts the resort had been tagged in. With no surprise, he noted that a number of them included details of Paige's dash from the altar and pictures of her puny fiancé looking downtrodden under an arch of monstera leaves.

It had taken himself and two of the maintenance boys an entire morning to craft that arch. He growled now, thinking of all the time and effort that had been wasted because Paige's fame-hungry former fiancé couldn't appreciate the gem he had in her.

*Imagine that arsehole thinking he could do better.*

Perhaps she'd been different in New Zealand. Perhaps in Paige's real life she was dramatic, emotional, difficult to be with. That incident on his porch before they'd kissed had hinted at a deeper well of feelings than he'd seen her display so far. Still, as someone who'd come face-to-face with the realisation that his own marriage had been built on a lie of love, he had little respect for the man who'd been willing to trick an unsuspecting fiancée into marital farce. Arranged marriages existed – and were successful – for a reason, but at least everyone in those knew what they were getting themselves into. Being blindsided by the revelation that your chosen life partner not only didn't love you, but didn't even like you? Mareko shook his head. Paige deserved better than that. *He* had deserved better than that. Even if fate and a drunk driver had ensured he was the single person alive who knew the truth – that Hélène had been leaving him – it didn't soften the blow.

Taking a break from the tiny square pictures of his family's resort that crowded his screen, he stared out at the staff garden, starting when his door burst open and his daughter flew in like a hurricane, throwing herself into one of the chairs in front of his desk in tears.

*What's wrong? Where is Paige?* The thought was through his head in an instant, but before he could even stand from his desk, she was there, arms around his daughter, rocking her gently from side to side.

"It's not fair," Rosa sobbed, and Mareko's heart caught in his chest, twisting tight at the sound of his daughter's anguish.

"I know it doesn't seem that way," Paige replied, her voice quieter. "Why don't you tell your dad about it?"

"I want to be a pastry chef." Rosa's volume increased, a sure sign of her anger. "Why won't Iosefa teach me how?"

Mareko opened his mouth, but nothing came out. Flailing, he caught Paige's eye and saw her empathy there.

"He is very skilled," Paige said, sympathetically, stroking a hand over Rosa's hair. "But perhaps he doesn't have the time to teach a new apprentice with all of the work he needs to produce for the resort?"

"If he trained me, I could help him." Rosa lifted her jaw stubbornly.

"What is it about being a pastry chef that you think you'd like best?" Paige slid into the chair, rearranging Rosa on her lap.

"I like puddings," Rosa ticked off one of her fingers. "Also, he's really busy and probably needs some help. Plus, then I could work for the resort, like you, Papa. We could work here together."

Mareko closed his eyes briefly against the hopeful gleam in his daughter's eyes, but the image struck him all the same. His baby, all grown up, whipping up confections in the resort kitchen in chef whites. He could practically taste the sugar on his tongue, hear the whip of coconut custard. But one cold thought stopped him. He'd never once heard Rosa mention working for the resort before. That was *his* dream. In fact, none of the reasons Rosa had given had to do with a desire to create desserts. If Rosa followed him into the resort business merely to make him happy, he'd never be able to forgive himself. The idea of her hunched over a desk, crunching numbers or slaving away over a hot stove to try and make him happy while her own dreams withered on the vine left a sour taste in his mouth.

"I see." Paige's voice was soft and when Mareko opened his eyes, he saw that she'd begun braiding Rosa's hair. "Well, if you want to be a pastry chef here, then that's what we'll do. If your dad doesn't object, of course."

"Of course not," Mareko croaked out. "Anything you want, Rosa."

"How?" Rosa wailed, her voice rising again. "Iosefa already said no!"

Paige shushed her gently. "There is always a way. Do you know how you eat an elephant, Rosa?"

"What?"

"Eating an elephant. Do you know how to?"

Confusion painted Rosa's features. "Do you... cook it on an umu?"

Paige grinned as she tied off the end of Rosa's braid, and Mareko's own lips lifted at the idea of an entire elephant being wrapped in taro leaves and roasted over a bed of hot rocks.

"Not quite." Paige pressed a kiss against the crown of Rosa's head. "You eat it one spoonful at a time."

"Huh?"

"You can't go straight into being Iosefa's apprentice. But you still want to get there, right?"

"Yes." His daughter's curiosity floated across the desk to Mareko and he was suffused with gratitude for Paige in this moment. He loved his daughter, beyond reason, but he'd never been comfortable with tears. They panicked him, whether they came from his child, his wife or his mother. Mareko was not a man of soft words and gentle discretion. He was a man of action. The impulse to order Iosefa into his office and demand he make Rosa his apprentice gnawed at him and he pushed it back, curious to see how Paige finagled this situation and somewhat in awe of her calm demeanour in the face of Rosa's dramatics.

"So, we need to break your goal down into smaller tasks. What are his easiest desserts? We can learn how to make those, one at a time. I'll help you practise each day. Then we move onto the harder ones, or the more popular ones. You're learning the skills he would need you to have to let you help out in the kitchen, and you're also proving that you're committed to the work. Here–" Mareko watched as Paige shifted under Rosa in the seat, pulling her phone out of the pocket of her denim cutoffs "– we can make a spreadsheet of the skills and recipes you'll need to learn, and a schedule for achieving them. How does that sound?"

"That sounds really good," Rosa acknowledged. "Can you show me how to make a spreadsheet too? That way I can keep working on it when you leave."

"Of course I can." Paige pulled Rosa into a hug and Mareko suddenly felt the need to go to them, to wrap both of them in his arms as they sat, heads together, light and dark cocooned within the heart of The Moananui. The unfamiliar longing tugged at him even as Paige coaxed Rosa back towards the kitchens to apologise for running out on Iosefa, both waving goodbye to him while Rosa blew him a kiss and Paige mouthed a 'Sorry for interrupting' over his daughter's head.

*She's perfect*, he realised. Not dramatic, not emotional. Smart and pragmatic. No conversation involving a spreadsheet should have turned him on so effectively, no incident involving his child's tears should have either, but it had. Mareko had never doubted Paige's ability to be an exceptional nanny for Rosa – her qualifications check had been quick but thorough. But seeing her balance his daughter's impromptu outburst with logic and practicality made him think that she met all the criteria to be a perfect match for him as well. He pressed his lips into a grim line as he stood and moved to open one of the windows.

Breathing in the floral air, the thought shook him. Seemingly perfect or not, he could not afford to make a mistake about the next woman he took into his bed. His lustful impulses had led him astray before and he was still trying to unpick the damage they had left in their wake.

*No*, Mareko thought, as he moved to his desk and picked up his reports again. *She's leaving. No amount of spreadsheets or baking is going to change that.*

The best thing to do – the *only* thing to do – was to maintain his distance from her. If he didn't see her too much, speak to her too much, then his lust would abate. It must. Logic dictated it.

Holidays, Paige decided, were the best.

She hadn't had many, not with all her hospital stays, and going directly to university after high school before medical training. After that, it had been work, floundering to keep her head above water as a general practitioner registrar in New Zealand's permanently stretched healthcare system. Since she worked in the town closest to her parent's farm, she'd often volunteered to work over Christmas and the summer holidays so other members of staff could visit families flung further afield than the twenty-minute drive to her parent's place. But the last couple of weeks had convinced her. She needed more holidays.

Not that she was sunning herself on the beach twenty-four seven. Rosa's pastry chef plan had been as educational for Paige as it had been for her charge. By now, they were both practically masters at macarons, and their custard cream pie had been given a hearty seal of approval from Penina. Well, the second one had. Their initial attempt at shortcrust pastry left a bit to be desired.

But in between the hours in the kitchen, there were moments like this that were absolute perfection.

"Thank you, Sione," Paige sang as she accepted a tall glass filled to the brim with a frothy fruit smoothie. She was perched up at the poolside bar, e-reader in hand and getting her money's worth out of the itsy-bitsy bikini she'd bought for the honeymoon that had never happened. There might be a lavalava covering most of the swimsuit – this was a public bar, after all – but at least she was wearing it.

"Anytime, Miss Paige," Sione the bartender replied easily. Rosa had been introducing her to the staff slowly over the last two weeks and Paige never failed to experience a spark of pleasure at how welcome everyone had made her feel to The Moananui Resort family.

To say nothing of how welcome Rosa and Penina had

made her feel. Mareko still kept his distance – not that she could blame him after she'd thrown herself at him – but his mother and daughter never treated her with anything other than warmth and kindness, Rosa often acting as a translator between her grandmother and her nanny. The easy acceptance of the Osa family was a direct contrast to her own upbringing – between the circumstances of her conception, her health issues as a young child and the expectations of her parents to achieve once she recovered, she was revelling in the opportunity to live a few weeks without feeling like eyes were on her. In many ways, the Osa family remind her of Patrick's parents. Although they'd met under strange circumstances, under the glare of lights with cameras capturing their every expression and editing it to suit Natalia's narrative vision, the Winslows had been approachable and down-to-earth. Paige had been looking forward to having them as in-laws.

As the cool fruitiness of the smoothie slid down her throat, Paige could admit to herself that while she felt foolish when she replayed Patrick's unkind comments about her, she was more disappointed that his revelations had cost her the chance to be a part of his family than she was about the furore that her runaway bride act had created. Part of her wanted to reach out to the Winslows and apologise, but she had no idea if they wanted to hear from her.

"What are you thinking about? You look too serious." Rosa plopped down on the bar stool next to Paige and tipped her chin at Sione. "Hit me."

"Please," Paige and Sione reminded her in unison.

"Hit me please, Sione," Rosa amended, batting her eyelashes at the burly bartender who shook his head and headed towards the smoothie bench.

"I'm thinking about families," Paige admitted as the blender roared to life behind her.

"What about them?"

"How different they all are. What I want my own family to look like."

Rosa nodded solemnly, her dark eyes never leaving Paige's as she took a sip from the papaya-coconut concoction that had appeared in front of her.

"Fa'afetai, Sione," she thanked him. "Do you want children?" Rosa fired the question at Paige who shrugged, discomfort pricking across her shoulders as she stirred her straw in the remains of her Green-a Colada. While Rosa was certainly mature for her age, there was something pathetic about admitting her failed dreams to a nine-year-old.

"I do," she said at last. She hadn't lied to Rosa about anything so far. This certainly wasn't the issue to start with. "I thought I was going to have them with Patrick. I know I'm not too old to have them yet, but my mother had trouble having babies so I need to consider that it might not happen easily for me."

"You could adopt," Rosa suggested. "Or marry someone who already has kids."

"All good options," Paige agreed, forcing her lips into a smile for Rosa's sake. She didn't say what she was thinking – that being loved was her priority. She wasn't a silly woman – she knew logically that biology played no real part in loving relationships, but the churn of her gut whispered to her that her own baby would love her unconditionally. A purer love than she could expect from a child with parents of their own, or even from her future partner. Patrick's willingness to start a family had been one of the reasons she'd fallen for him so quickly, despite his off-putting style of eating eggs. Though how much of that he'd meant was anyone's guess.

"Do you have kids, Sione?" Deflection, Paige decided, was almost as grand as a holiday.

"Four boys, two girls, one fa'afafine." Sione confirmed as he rinsed glasses behind the bar.

Paige gaped at him. "*Seven* children? Your poor wife."

"Poor me," Sione sighed. "The littlest one threw a shoe at me this morning. So much spirit. Like her mother." He shook his head. "Good when she grows up, but not much fun now."

Rosa snickered behind her glass and his eyes sparked as they landed on her. "Like you, yes, Miss Rosa?"

"Sione, I am a delight and a joy!" Rosa protested, a giggle escaping her rosebud lips.

"You are trouble, you are. You and my Ymania."

"Ymania is in my class at school," Rosa informed Paige. "She was born with boy parts but she's a girl. Last year we were in choir together."

"Does she like ABBA too?"

Rosa wrinkled her nose and shook her head. "She likes church songs the most."

Sione flicked a towel towards her. "You could use more church in your life, little one."

"I go on Sundays!"

"Samoans should go every day."

"I'm French, though."

Sione clutched his chest and staggered backwards. "Sacrilege!" Over the sound of Rosa's laughter, he turned to face Paige. "Being born in France is no reason to consider oneself French, is it?"

Paige lifted a shoulder. "She does make a mean macaron," she joked.

Sione sighed. "Wait until Mr Osa hears of this."

"No, don't tell him," Rosa bubbled, her eyes shining with glee. "I'm Samoan, Sione, I promise!"

"French!" Sione rolled his eyes. "The very idea…"

"I promise, Sione. I'm a good Samoan girl." Rosa twinkled up at the bartender, and Paige was once again struck by how the entire resort staff had adopted Rosa as their own, teasing and caring for her. What must that be like? To have an entire team of people who would envelope you as one of theirs, no questions asked? A cynic might point out that Rosa's acceptance might be reliant on her being the owner's daughter, but nobody could witness Rosa with the staff and think that they loved her for anything other than exactly who she was – a bright, funny, caring girl. Even a week ago when the pastry chef Iosefa had been explaining that she was unable to work in the resort's kitchen as his assistant, his smooth features had crinkled in distress at disappointing the girl.

That reminded her…

"What are we making today, Rosa?" Paige asked as Sione moved further down the bar to serve a customer.

"Today we're doing cheesecake." Rosa had been updating her spreadsheet as they mastered each item on the resort's dessert menu and checking which ingredients they'd need the next day. "Iosefa's speciality is the baked ginger caramel cheesecake, so we're trying that first."

"Ambitious. I love it."

"Also, Tinamatua wants to make some panipopo to take to Tamamatua when she visits tomorrow. I said we'd help her with that." Rosa slurped the last of her drink.

"What are panipopo?" Paige asked. So far they'd avoided tackling traditional desserts, given the resort kitchen's efforts to appeal to the global palate of its international guests.

"Coconut buns," Rosa licked her lips dramatically. "They're the best."

Paige smiled. "They sound delicious. I can't wait. What time do you want to start?"

Rosa's brow furrowed as she snuck a glance over at the clock behind the bar. "Let's start at two. That gives us time for one more swim."

"You go ahead," Paige waved her off. "I'm going to read for a little bit and work on my tan." She gestured to where their bags were sitting beside the blue-cushioned poolside loungers. "You'll be okay?"

"Yup!" Rosa bounded off and Paige watched as she executed a perfect swan dive into the pool. It wasn't deep, and Rosa was tall for her age – she could easily touch the bottom, as evidenced by the fact that her skinny brown legs immediately popped up out of the blue as she performed an underwater handstand.

"She is lovely, isn't she?"

Paige turned to see Sione smiling towards the pool indulgently. "She is so kind to my Ymania," he continued. "Fa'afafine have always been part of Samoan culture but as the islands get more access to the world through the Internet, some of the world's ideas about gender reach us too. They are not always positive." He shook his head sadly. "Rosa, though, she is the first one to stand up for Ymania if she is having problems at school."

Paige's heart ached for Sione's little girl even as it swelled with pride for Rosa.

"She is incredible," she agreed, watching as Rosa performed a length of dolphin dives down the pool. "If I could be guaranteed children like her, I might consider seven of them myself."

Sione chuckled lightly. "If they were all like her, I might

try to convince my wife we need eight." He laughed harder when Paige winced. "I have been watching you with her this week, Miss Paige. You will be a wonderful mother. Any child would be lucky to have you."

Warmth that had nothing to do with the tropical climate bloomed over Paige's cheeks. "Thank you, Sione," she offered quietly. "I hope they feel the same way when the time comes."

*I hope the time actually comes*, she thought. But she kept that thought to herself. The Moananui Resort staff had already been first hand witnesses to one of her dreams being shattered. There was no need to give them a checklist of the rest, which seemed less and less obtainable with each passing day.

"Did you put that on my tab?"

Paige looked up in surprise. Mareko leaned against the polished wooden bar, looking for all the world like a supermodel. His grey suit jacket hugged his strong arms, the white of his shirt playing up his tan skin. Dark eyes pinned her in place and Paige's heart fluttered at being the sole object of his focus.

"Of course not," she managed, quickly arranging her towel across her lap in an attempt to seem more professional. Had she finished rubbing in her sunscreen? As discreetly as possible, she ran her fingers over her cheek, swiping away the creamy film of residue. "I can pay for my own drinks. It's non-alcoholic," she added hurriedly.

Mareko shrugged. "All employees have tabs. You're here looking after Rosa. You should be putting it on my tab."

"That's kind of you, but I'm happy to pay."

"Nonsense. Sione!"

"Yes, boss?"

"Please make sure all of Miss Beckett's drinks are put on my tab from now on."

"Of course, boss." Sione shot Paige a cheeky wink.

Mareko's jaw tightened. "Enough of that, Sione." He watched the other man walk towards the back of the bar. "Everyone is being helpful?"

Paige nodded vigorously as she took a sip of her drink. "Everyone has been wonderful," she assured him as she swallowed. "I'm so grateful to all of the staff."

"Excellent." His eyes seemed to linger on her lips, and Paige swallowed again. Hard. For a fleeting moment she wished she'd worn a cover up that did a little more covering up of her honeymoon bikini, maybe slicked on a little tinted lip balm. Mareko always looked like such a professional. It was slightly intimidating. Especially now, with her hair bundled into a hasty bun, her nails chipped. She looked as much a mess on the outside as she was on the inside.

"Ooh, Papa!" Rosa was back, and Mareko dragged his eyes down the length of Paige's body before settling on his daughter. A shiver ran through Paige in response. "Are you having lunch with us?"

"I'm afraid not, afa'fine." Mareko tucked a strand of his daughter's wet hair behind her ear. "I am here to take a few photos of Sione and the bar." Catching Paige's eye, he shrugged. "I am now in charge of our social media marketing as well."

Rosa pouted. "Boring."

Mareko smiled indulgently, and Paige's heart clenched at the clear bond between the two of them. She longed for that with her own child one day.

"Boring, but necessary. And what is this I hear about you letting Paige buy her own drinks? She should be putting them on my tab."

"I thought she was!" Rosa turned to Paige. "Are you buying them yourself? Stop it this instant. What kind of hosts do you think we are?"

"I'm not a guest," Paige pointed out. "I'm an employee, and I'm happy to pay my way while I'm here."

Mareko moved closer, even as Rosa waved an imperious hand to dismiss Paige's statement.

"Don't," he murmured, his voice low enough for only her to hear. "I want to be the one to buy your drinks."

With a light sweep of his hand against the small of her back, he was gone, and Paige was left melting in ways that had nothing to do with the heat.

# CHAPTER 6

"*I*t's really more of a deep tissue massage."

"My hands are so sticky. Do I scrape it off and stick it back in?"

"Pretty much."

"Well, that doesn't seem sanitary."

"You washed your hands, it's fine. Otherwise there'll be no dough left."

Mareko grinned to himself at his daughter's firm instruction as he climbed the bungalow's porch steps, the sunset streaking orange and pink across the sky behind him. Whatever was happening at the moment, Rosa was most definitely in charge.

Stepping into the kitchen, he stopped dead. Nothing could have prepared him.

It wasn't the flour spread across the stainless-steel counter that rattled him, or the thick, sticky-looking mass of dough – bread for panipopo, if he wasn't mistaken – that left his throat dry. It wasn't the overpowering scent of fresh ginger. It wasn't even the humidity, although he'd be more comfortable blaming the sudden perspiration on his brow on that.

It was Paige. Decked out in a yellow bikini, she smiled down at his daughter. Her hands were covered in bread dough, her silver-blonde hair piled up in a messy topknot.

And her body.

Gods help him, her body.

Her breasts were small but high, lovingly cupped by the yellow fabric of her swimsuit and kept in place by the flimsiest ties he'd ever laid eyes on. And he'd worked at resorts the world over. Although not overly tall, her body was compact, with a smooth stomach and thick thighs that she'd so far kept under wraps with long skirts and dresses.

He wanted to run his hands over every inch of it.

"Mareko?" His mother's voice interrupted his train of thought as swiftly and effectively as a bucket of cold water.

"Tina?" he responded. Out of the corner of his eye he saw Paige hurriedly wash her hands and move towards the couch to grab a lavalava in a pretty purple and turquoise print. She wrapped it around herself quickly, securing it in a common wrap style used by Samoan women. It was for the best. He'd faltered today already, only days after swearing to keep his distance from Paige. He'd seen her at the bar and told her how much he wanted to be the one taking care of her while she relaxed. But Gods, how could he help himself? She was temptation personified, and he struggled to hold Penina's gaze instead of looking his fill of the woman who had thrown him for a loop.

Penina gave him the type of side eye only a mother could, and Mareko concentrated hard on last month's budget reports to stop a flush creeping up his neck. She opened her mouth, but his phone rang in his pocket.

"Tulou," he excused himself, fishing it out and thumbing to accept the call from the unfamiliar number. "Talofa lava."

"Mr Osa? This is Aisi from Tupua Tamasese Meaole Hospital." The speaker used Samoan, and a calm cadence that immediately raised the hair on the back of Mareko's neck.

"What's wrong?" He snapped the words out in his native language. His family's heads snapped up as his harsh tone bounced off the kitchen walls, but he was focused on the call.

"I'm afraid your father suffered a medical incident at his residential care facility. He was transferred to our intensive care unit approximately half an hour ago after suffering a cardiac arrest in transit."

Mareko was already moving, grabbing his keys off the hook by the refrigerator. "Sau," he called to his family, as his eyes roamed over Paige.

*Paige.*

*Doctor Beckett.*

She must have heard something in his voice, because she was already helping Rosa with her shoes, murmuring soothing comfort to the girl as she asked what was going on. Even as he watched, Paige located his mother's purse and handed it to her.

"You too," he commanded in English, and her eyes met his. There was empathy there, swirling in their emerald depths and he knew that she knew. "Come with us. Please. Is he okay now?" He spoke back into the phone as he exited the bungalow and shoved his feet into his shoes.

"He is being prepped for surgery," the calm voice replied.

"We'll be there in ten minutes." It was a twenty-minute

drive but he would run every blasted red light in Apia if he had to.

Fear gripped his heart. Not his tama. He had to be alright. He had to.

They bundled into the resort van that was parked on a small dirt track that ran around the back of the house and he gunned it down the private back road that led directly to the city.

Twelve minutes later they reached the hospital and Mareko forced himself to park carefully in one of the designated parking areas rather than screeching to a stop in front of the main doors.

The smell hit him instantly - institution and antiseptic. The last time he'd been in a hospital had been the night Hélène died, and he fought back the tide of nausea that rose in his throat.

*He'll be okay. He'll be okay.* He had to be okay.

Mareko power-walked to the reception desk with Rosa at his side, while Paige bundled Penina into a wheelchair by the entrance on account of her bad leg, and was informed that his father was likely to be in the operating theatre for a further hour or so. They piled into the waiting room, where Mareko paced and his mother prayed. Rosa sat silently, her eyes wide with worry as they darted between the two of them. Paige fetched coffees from the hospital cafe along with small bags of homemade taro chips that Rosa devoured. Finally, long after the artificial chill of the hospital had settled in Mareko's chest, a doctor arrived in the doorway.

"Mr Osa?"

"That's me," Mareko replied in Samoan, moving quickly to stand in front of the other man. "How is my father?"

The doctor eyed him solemnly. "Your father is alive, but

unwell. We have inserted stents to prevent further narrowing of the arteries and increase blood flow. Due to his advanced age, recuperation is likely to be slow and he may never completely recover."

Behind him, his mother gasped out a sob and he heard Rosa murmuring assurances to her grandmother.

"Can we see him?" Desperation to see his father, to hold his hand and witness the spark of life within his eyes, clawed at Mareko.

"Briefly. He is in recovery at the moment, but will be moved to a private room as soon as possible." The doctor gave Mareko a meaningful look, and he realised that an offering would be necessary to ensure his father the privacy of a single room. No matter. A small payment was nothing to ensure his father's stay was undisturbed by the unpredictable comings and goings of others.

"I understand," Mareko nodded. "Who should I speak to about that?"

The doctor's lips tugged upwards briefly. An understanding had been reached. "Nurse Pao will arrange something. He should be at the nurse's station." The doctor's eyes flicked over Mareko's shoulder. "At this stage, only family is permitted visitation rights."

*Like hell.* If Mareko had unlimited access to a doctor during his father's health crisis he was undoubtedly going to take advantage of it.

"Miss Beckett is my fiancée," he lied firmly, ignoring the way his mother's breath hitched behind him. A second later, Penina began reciting the rosary, though whether it was for his sin of lying or in hope it was true, he couldn't say.

The doctor's brow rose, but he nodded. "Your father will likely be ready to return to the ward within an hour. I suggest you speak to Nurse Pao and get something to eat.

There will be many meetings in the coming days around your father's health journey." He placed a hand on Mareko's shoulder. "It would not do for any of your family to lose sight of their own health under the strain. Your father will need the strength of his aiga if he hopes to improve."

Mareko nodded, the mantle of responsibility heavy on his shoulders. Already the list of things he needed to organise swelled to epic proportions in his head, a black hole that stretched outward and drained him of energy. Penina would want to be by Enele's side as he recovered. If he were honest with himself, Mareko did too. But there was the resort to consider – and fire burned bright in his gut at that thought. His father was alive, and that was enough for now, but Mareko vowed that Enele Osa would see The Moananui restored to its rightful place as a jewel in the crown of Samoan tourism before he was called to Heaven.

*Thank the gods for Paige. At least Rosa will be taken care of in the madness that we're facing.*

Giving his head a slight shake, he forced a smile onto his face and turned back towards his family.

"He is alive and stable. That is good news."

Rosa threw herself at him, her thin arms wrapping tightly around Mareko's midsection and squeezing. Muffled sobs racked her body.

"There, there," Mareko murmured, stroking her hair ineffectually. He wanted to crouch, to scoop her up into the safety of his arms and hold her there where sadness and hurt couldn't breach his protection. She was wound too tightly around him to even squat down to eye level though. Instead, he continued to smooth his hand over her hair, slow rhythmic strokes as her small form shuddered. Rosa had barely slept in the year following Hélène's death. To lose another family member so soon would devastate her.

Hell, it would devastate him. He was only thirty-one – far too young to be without his tama. And his mother... he sought her out. The fluorescent lights painted her skin a sallow tone as she fingered the rosary beads he'd sent her from Vatican City. Her eyes were lowered, fixed on her task, but he could see the tracks of since-wiped tears clearly on her cheeks.

No, none of them were ready for Enele to leave this earth.

Pulling back slightly, he loosened Rosa's hold around his waist. "Would you like to go see your tamamatua when he gets back to his room?"

His daughter nodded, swiping her own tears away. "Yes, please."

"You stay with Tinamatua and Paige then, and I will go find out which room he will be in." He'd spotted an ATM machine in the foyer. Hopefully Nurse Pao was in a generous mood – most of Mareko's personal funds had gone into The Moananui's restoration and he was loath to borrow cash from the resort to cover bribes. It sat a little too close to the mismanagement of funds from Edwin, the previous general manager.

It turned out Nurse Pao was fairly receptive, and within ninety minutes they were in Enele's private room. Penina fussed around her husband, fluffing his pillows as though the hospital staff hadn't done a perfectly adequate job. Rosa held her grandfather's hand and told him all about making panipopo with Paige. Her voice was smaller than usual, worry etched into the downward tilt of her lips even as Enele laughed weakly at her description of Paige's hands covered in the sticky globs of bread dough.

Paige herself had tried to wait in the hall, but Mareko had gently steered her into the room with his hand on the small of her back. Despite the hospital's air conditioning, her skin was warm through the thin barrier of the lavalava she wore and Enele had greeted her warmly in Samoan, Mareko translating as she relayed her hopes for his swift recovery.

She sidled over to the wall as though she was trying to disappear – as if she could be in a room and he wouldn't notice her – but he motioned her over towards the bed with a quick flick of his head.

"I need your help," he murmured under his breath when she was in earshot.

"Anything." Her green eyes swam with empathy. She must be a wonderful doctor, he realised. Not merely competent, but her caring nature would shine through in every interaction she had with patients. He sincerely hoped his father received the kind of care Paige Beckett would provide. Speaking of...

"I'd like your thoughts on my father's condition."

Paie looked puzzled. "I don't have the details."

He tapped his finger against Enele's chart, which hung over the aluminium bar at the foot of the hospital bed.

"They're right here."

"In Samoan," she pointed out. "Which I don't speak."

"I can translate. Please," he added when she hesitated. "I won't hold you to anything, but I would like your perspective. I need to hear the details from someone I trust."

Saying the word aloud pinched in his chest, but he did trust her. Not simply as a medical professional, but as a person. She would be honest with him about Enele's condition. And then... then he would know for sure. How long he had left with his dear father. How long to restore The Moananui to glory, so his father would not leave this

Earth having seen a lifetime of his hard work crumpled into economic mediocrity.

The very idea of failing sent his stomach into freefall, a swirling nothingness that almost took his breath away. He could not – *would not* – fail.

"Please," he added again. "I need to know."

Biting her lip, Paige nodded cautiously. "I'm not a surgeon, Mareko. I can't promise I'll be of any use. But if you read the chart to me, I can tell you what I think."

Relief rushed out of him on an exhale. "Thank you."

Scooping up his father's chart, he led her out of the room to the hallway. The lights were dim to account for the late hour, with the exception of the nurses' station, which glowed like a beacon to their left. Mareko headed right, finding a small lounge at the end of the hall, lit by a single table lamp. He took a seat next to the light, Paige perching on an uncomfortable-looking seat across from him. He looked over at her. Despite her stature and the lush width of her hips, she looked small in the empty space. Her shoulders hunched as she ran the thumb of her right hand up and down over a scar he hadn't noticed before on the inside of her left bicep. Gooseflesh pebbled her skin, and he tried not to stare.

"Here." His voice was brusque as he shrugged off his suit jacket. He'd loosened his tie as they waited for news on Enele's condition, but he was still in his work clothes. He passed the jacket across to Paige, who he realised now still wore a swimsuit, flip flops and a lavalava. "You must be cold. Put this on."

"I'm okay."

"You're not. Do it for me," he requested, when she shot him an exasperated look. "I don't have the capacity to worry about anyone else right now."

Paige's jaw tightened, but she reached for the jacket and drew it on. "It's not the temperature," she muttered. "I don't like hospitals."

"You're a doctor, yes? How can you dislike hospitals?"

"I don't want to talk about it." She didn't meet his eyes. "What does your dad's chart say?"

Distracted from her bizarre statement, he glanced down at the chart on his lap. Flipping it open he ran through the notes inside – unfamiliar procedures, long-forgotten biological terms, lists of medication dosages and times – translating the Samoan to English and stumbling through the pharmaceutical jargon as he went.

Paige nodded every now and then, her eyes still downcast. But now her lack of eye contact seemed more based in concentration than avoidance. Her shoulders straightened and she sat back further in her seat as he read. By the time he reached the end of Enele's notes, her transformation from an unsure makeshift nanny into a competent doctor was complete.

"It sounds promising at this stage," she assured him, looking up now, and the confidence in her green eyes when she said it was a balm to his adrenaline-tight body. He sank back in his own chair as she explained the situation further, using layperson's terms. His father's life had been precariously in the balance, but the quick work of the hospital team had saved him and the prognosis for his recovery was tentatively positive.

*Better than tentatively*, Mareko thought fiercely. The doctors didn't know Enele Osa like he did. His father's resilience and grit had guided Mareko's whole life. If the doctors – including Paige – said Enele's odds were good, then he had to believe he would recover.

There was no other acceptable option.

PAIGE FOLLOWED Mareko back into his father's hospital room, stopping inside the door while he carried on towards the bed, kissing his father's cheek and joking with him about the scare he's given them. She could appreciate the effort he was making to ease his father's mind about the thick cloak of fear that had settled over every member of the Osa family when the phone call had come. Paige had seen her share of fear in her life. Professionally with patients, and personally with her parents. She recognised the signs – the tight pinch of worry at the corner of Mareko's mouth, the way the knuckles of his bronze skin whitened as he gripped his phone like a security blanket while pacing the waiting room. Even now that he sat on the edge of the bed chatting with Enele, his brows furrowed over his dark almond eyes in a way that betrayed his jovial tone.

Paige shivered, leaning against the cool wall. She hadn't known where she would end up when Mareko had ordered her to come with him. If she had, she might have resisted, though she would have struggled saying no when he turned that fear-filled gaze on her. She'd tried to make herself useful while they waited, fetching coffee and snacks. But eventually she'd run out of avoidance techniques, and then the chill had set in.

Her own fear was different to Mareko's, she knew that. His was in the moment, flaring hot and bright. An instantaneous reaction to a sudden threat. Hers was insidious, creeping in, wrapping itself tight around her and squeezing, constricting her airflow with cold fingers.

Mareko was right, it was a miracle she'd managed to finish her medical degree with her aversion towards hospitals hanging over her, but she'd been singularly motivated by her own fear of failure and the idea of being able to help others. To help them the way that she had needed help when she was younger. The pressure from her parents, the way they swelled with pride when telling people about her chosen career, that had helped keep her going on the dark days too. But she hadn't set foot in a hospital since the final day of her last training rotation, and she would have been happy to keep it that way.

Through the light fabric of Mareko's suit jacket, Paige traced the scar on her arm – a physical reminder of the cancer that had ravaged her young body and taken two years of battle to defeat. Her emotional wounds hadn't healed nearly so neatly. They still scarred her psyche – ugly, jagged pockmarks that caused her to push herself harder, to try to be better, to try to be *enough* to make up for the pain and suffering her parents had faced as their longed-for only child turned out to be deficient in health.

Yeah, her time in psych rotation hadn't been wasted, either.

Being on the opposite side of the hospital bed during her years of training had numbed her fears, but not alleviated them. She wished she could wait in the van, but Rosa kept throwing little glances her way and Mareko was gesturing towards her while he spoke in Samoan to his father, who smiled weakly at her under his oxygen cannula.

She couldn't leave. Not without seeming rude. Mareko and his family had done so much for her, helping her escape the travesty of her dramatic almost-wedding, giving her a job and a place to stay. If her presence was easing their burden in even the smallest way, she would stay. Even if unease prickled along her nerve endings and her breathing wasn't quite as deep and even as she would have liked.

Fortunately, the late hour encouraged the Osas to wrap

up their visit quickly, and Paige waited for them in the hall as they made what she guessed were promises to visit tomorrow, based on the rudimentary Samoan Rosa had taught her so far. The ride back to the resort was silent, everyone lost in their own thoughts. Penina and Rosa went to bed immediately, but Paige opted for a shower. Despite the warmth of the night air that flowed in through the bungalow windows, the chill of walking through halls that echoed her childhood trauma was still heavy in her bones.

She stood under the hot spray for a long time, letting the heat seep into her body and the steam envelop her until she could barely see. When she shut the water off, her head was calmer, clearer. Padding through the bungalow wrapped in a towel, Paige made it to her bedroom and pulled her phone off the charger where she'd placed it while she and Rosa attempted to make panipopo earlier in the evening.

It felt like weeks ago.

Paige knew better than most how a medical diagnosis could seem to alter time. To slow it down, speed it up, spin you around until you had no concept of it – until your days were measured in pills and needles rather than hours and minutes. And that most people felt towards the end that they hadn't had enough of it.

With that thought in mind, she pulled up her mother's number and pressed the call button.

"Hello?"

"Hi Mum, it's me. I'm sorry about the late hour." There was no time difference between Samoa and New Zealand, but Kathleen Beckett had always had firm views on the rudeness of calling people between nine at night and nine in the morning, and Paige was definitely in that window.

"Paige?" There was a rustling noise which Paige assumed was Kathleen sitting up in bed.

"Yup."

"It's late. Is everything alright?"

"Yes, everything's fine. I just–" Paige blew out a breath. Knowing she needed to apologise didn't make doing so any easier "– I'm calling to say sorry about the wedding."

Her mother sniffed and the clear sound of disappointment floated through the earpiece and settled over Paige like a cloud. "What on Earth happened? Everyone was looking for you."

"Yes. I know."

"Bad enough that you went on that terrible show in the first place. The way they made you look–"

"I know, Mum." The show's editors had not been kind.

"Then to have all those people running around looking for you, only to find you'd disappeared. Do you have any idea how much panic you caused?"

"I know." Paige was repeating herself, but there was nothing else to say. Pressure built behind her skull.

"The magazines keep ringing now. Showing up at the farm to try and ask us questions. People keep stopping me in the street and I have no idea what to tell them." Her mother's voice cracked, and the first tear fell, landing on Paige's thigh. She watched dispassionately as it rolled down her pink, damp skin, eventually soaking into the cream linen coverlet. She swiped the next few away.

*Why did I call?*

"I'm sorry for all of that, Mum. I did what I thought was best at the time."

"Best for who? Paige, if something was wrong, you needed to tell us. We're not mind readers. After everything this family has been through–"

"I have to go," Paige interrupted. She couldn't hear this, not now. The story of how much she'd been wanted had been pulled out and twirled around her regularly growing up. Every time she was a little too loud, a little too wild. The one time she failed a chemistry test, the two times she failed her driver's licence test. At every opportunity to remind her that her parents loved her, but they loved her more when she was perfect. That Kathleen had given up her own career when Paige's failing health had impeded on their vision of family life. Her parents had longed for a child, but Paige had wondered more than once if they regretted the fact that she was the embryo selected. Perhaps a different child would have been healthier. Happier. Better at chemistry, or driving.

"I'll talk to you later, Mum. Give Dad my love."

She hung up, shaking. Stared down at her hands, the perfect soft pink of her wedding-day manicure flaked and ravaged after almost two weeks of swimming and baking with Rosa.

*Perhaps I'll get my nails done tomorrow.* She clung to the trivial thought, holding it in the forefront of her mind, over the hollow fallout of her call home. She'd always been jealous of her flatmate Lily's nails, which were constantly painted vibrant colours. Between the amount of time Paige spent wearing gloves and her usual low-maintenance style, having her nails done had pretty much been reserved for special occasions like her graduation or wedding. Even on *One True Love*, Natalia had encouraged her to embrace 'the more natural look' compared to some of the other contestants. Well, she was miles from her doctor's surgery, miles from Natalia and her parent's disappointment and Lily's stash of nail colours, so she was going to do it, she decided firmly. She never seemed to make anyone happy as it was, but pretty nails? That would make Paige happy, and that might be enough right now.

"Paige?" Mareko's voice floated through the dark wood of her bedroom door.

"Yes?" She sat up straighter on the bed, securing her towel tightly around herself.

"Are you okay?"

Paige huffed out an incredulous laugh. "Are you?"

A pause, then, "Not really."

"Me neither."

"Can I come in?"

"Sure. It's your house."

Her dark wood bedroom door swung open, and then Mareko was there, backlit from the living room, tie discarded, shirtsleeves rolled up, his usually tidy hair rumpled as though he'd been running his hands through it. He looked at her and for an instant Paige could see everything in his eyes. Fear and guilt and hope and confusion.

"Oh, honey," she sighed, and opened her arms. He was in them in an instant.

"I'm sorry," he said, his voice muffled by her shoulder. "I'm sorry, I need a second."

"Don't worry about it." She held him tighter, as though she could keep him safe from the struggles that were coming. She stroked the short hair at the back of his neck and hummed gently when his torso rose and fell with deep breaths. The muscles across his shoulders were taut and her fingers brushed under the collar of his shirt, trailing her fingers over his warm skin. He sighed against her neck, and the tension slowly leaked out of him.

"Better?" she asked when he pulled back, and he nodded.

"What about you?" The question caught her off guard,

but he raised one hand to her face and traced his thumb along the delicate skin under her eye. "You've been crying."

"Ah. That." Paige forced her lips into a rueful smile. "I rang my mother after we got back from the hospital. Your father's condition puts things in perspective for me, I suppose. But I think they're angry about the wedding."

Mareko lifted one dark brow. "Your parents think you should have married someone who didn't love you?"

"They don't know that," Paige confessed. "They think I changed my mind. My parents don't like being disappointed, and this whole thing – the reality show, the engagement, the failed wedding – I've disappointed them at every stage of it. I've *embarrassed* them. I've embarrassed myself, too, I suppose. The tears... I guess I wish sometimes that supporting me came before their pride. Even when I'm doing the wrong thing."

"Leaving that man was not the wrong thing," Mareko growled, and she shrugged.

"Being with him in the first place was the wrong thing, though. I've tried so hard to live up to my parents' expectations for me. High marks in school, going into medicine. I've always been scared I'll make the wrong decision and let them down, so they made a lot of my decisions for me. When I heard about the show I thought, 'finally. I might meet someone who will love me for who I am, not what I can achieve.'" She shrugged. "Maybe that sounds naïve, thinking that reality television would represent me the way I am. But it's hard to meet someone in a small town where I work fourteen hours a day. I thought this would expedite the process. My parents had been mentioning grandchildren, and honestly," she sighed, closing her eyes, Mareko running his thumb across her cheek, "honestly, I just wanted to feel loved."

"He made you feel that way?" Markeo's voice was tight.

"He made me feel like I was enough. And that was almost as good as being loved." Paige sighed, the stress of the evening stripping her back to honesty. "But it turns out even that was a lie. I wasn't enough for him."

"Paige." A thread of urgency ran through Mareko's tone.

"Yes?" She opened her eyes and he was there, his handsome face inches from hers, hand still cupping her cheek.

"I have told you before, and I will tell you as many times as it takes for you to believe it. You. Are. Enough. Anyone who can't see that is a fool."

Then his mouth was on hers, hot and sweet, the taste of coffee lingering on his tongue when he licked between her lips.

She opened her mouth on a moan, and he kissed her again. Deeper than before, hungrier. On a subconscious level Paige knew he was trying to forget, trying to blur away the pain and panic of the last few hours but she didn't care. She could be that for him. Now, at this moment, she *was* enough.

She was enough when Mareko dropped his head to press kisses against her shoulder. She was enough when he murmured her name and pressed her back onto the bed. She was enough when he unwrapped her towel, leaving her bare, and kissed across her breasts.

Mareko caressed her curves, squeezing them in his big hands. She gasped his name into the air as he tugged one aching tip into his mouth, savouring her. Paige reached out, tangling her fingers in his thick air, holding on for dear life as he sucked and laved, pleasure mounting in her, twisting into a pointed throb that reverbed from her breasts to the empty space between her thighs.

"You taste good," Mareko murmured, and she grunted in response.

*Elegant.* But there was no point trying to walk it back now, and Mareko didn't even appear to have noticed, he was focusing so intently on her nipples, drawing one deeply into his mouth while he ran his thumb back and forth across the other.

"I've been dying to see these," he murmured across her skin, biting the curve of one breast gently and Paige gasped, bucking against the leg he'd worked between her thighs, searching for the friction to send her higher.

"You need more, beautiful?"

"Yes, please."

Mareko moved lower, pressing her thighs apart, leaving her naked and exposed while he hovered fully dressed above her. The dichotomy drove Paige wild, weeks worth of anticipation and sexual tension twisting through her bloodstream, the haze of lust descending until everything else faded away and there was nothing but Mareko, with his dark head between her legs, looking at her pussy like it was the Holy Grail.

Then he dipped his head and licked her, bottom to top, finishing with a light suckling kiss on her clit and Paige bit her own forearm to keep from screaming.

*Holy crap.* His mouth was a miracle. He did it again, that full swipe that covered her intimately, and again, the sweet suction of his lips on the tender bud of nerves like an exclamation point punctuating her desire. It was clearly working, she was more desperate than she'd ever been, and God love him, he didn't deviate from what was clearly working.

Time and time again, his mouth moved over her, wrenching the glittering parachute in her stomach tighter as he shoved her towards the cliff. And then, when she was almost there, he shoved two fingers deep inside her, curling them, and concentrating on her clit, and sensation rocked her as she tumbled over the edge, white-hot bolts of electricity surging up her spine and out to her limbs, her thighs clenching around his head to hold him in place as she fractured, bright shards of pleasure exploding out from her body as she rode his face and screamed into her elbow before collapsing back against the pillows as the fireworks inside her faded to a slow swirl of glitter flittering through darkness behind her closed lids.

"Again," Mareko said, and she batted a hand lazily in his direction without opening her eyes.

"Soon."

"Now, Paige." And then his hands were under her arse, tilting and lifting her closer to his face, and his lips were exploring her again, gently, taking care not to put too much pressure on her still-sensitive clit, and there was no more soon, there was only more. More sensation. More lust. More tightening of her inner muscles as he loved her with his tongue and built her up again, spilling tender words about how delicious she tasted into the warm air above them.

In the moment before she exploded for a second time, Paige knew that although Mareko had come seeking comfort from her, each intentional stroke of his tongue was his way of making sure that she learnt to believe what he'd said.

*You are enough.*

# CHAPTER 7

"No. Absolutely not. That's not happening."

"Why not?" Mareko asked.

"Why not?" Paige's look was incredulous. She turned to Rachel, who leaned in the doorway. "Are you hearing this?"

Rachel shook her head. "Unbelievable."

"Other resorts do this kind of thing all the time."

"Other resorts are tacky and cheap. Do you want people to think The Moananui is tacky and cheap?"

Well, no, that was the exact opposite of what Mareko wanted. But still...

"Research shows that, with the right advertising, just one bikini contest can bring in enough revenue to sustain a week's staffing costs."

Rachel, evidently fed up with his stupidity, interjected at this point. "Mareko. I will not work at a place that objectifies women. I don't care how much money it generates. You should be ashamed of yourself for suggesting it."

Mareko sighed. "It was an idea."

"It was a terrible one," his concierge assured him.

"I can see that now." He certainly could. Paige and

Rachel were both looking at him like he'd suggested an afternoon of kicking puppies. In truth, the idea of hosting a bikini contest at the resort had scraped his nerves, but the financial benefits were too lucrative not to consider. And after last night, he couldn't deny that he liked having Paige's attention on him. He'd made love with women before, but sinking into Paige Beckett for the first time last night had been like a baptism. He felt reborn. It had taken everything in him to drag himself from her bed as thin streaks of dawn lit the sky this morning and he'd been counting down the minutes until he could return home to her. Fortunately, she'd appeared like a vision in his office doorway moments ago. Unfortunately, it had been while he was brainstorming revenue avenues with Rachel. It was something, he supposed, that the two women seemed to get on so well, though he would prefer it that they did not aim their collective ire at him.

"We have the fiafia night on Sundays," Rachel reminded him. "Palagi love the traditional dancers and the feast. No offence," she added, looking at Paige, who shrugged.

"None taken. It sounds brilliant."

Rachel nodded. "Perhaps we could consider adding an additional session on Wednesdays? We could rotate the dancers week on, week off to save them from burnout."

Mareko nodded, running a hand across his chin as he pulled his attention from the delicate curve of Paige's neck to refocus on what Rachel was saying. It wasn't a bad idea. The fiafia nights were successful - visitors came from other resorts and private accommodation on the island to watch local dancers perform, tucking into full roasted pigs and palusami – taro leaves cooked in coconut – while the sound of traditional wooden drums filled the night air and siva afi – firesticks – spun around them in the talented hands of the performers. The dances were taxing though, particularly on the men, who tended to perform more high-energy routines than the gentle sensuality of the traditionally female dances. Alternating weeks would ensure they were paid the same as their current earnings while ensuring they didn't become too tired to perform.

"That's a great idea," he admitted. "Would it be possible to get all the dancers in for a meeting this afternoon to gauge interest?" Most of the performers worked at The Moananui in different capacities, but several held jobs outside the resort – fishermen and women, teachers, and a lone tax lawyer.

Rachel nodded. "I'll do my best." She disappeared towards her own office and Mareko turned to Paige.

*Gods, she's pretty.* Her hair was down, tousled in damp waves as it dried around her face. She must have been swimming recently. She was wearing another one of her floaty sundresses and it was all he could do not to drop to his knees and bury his face between her thighs under the fabric.

"Did you have a reason for stopping by, other than to critique my management style?" He ensured his voice stayed light, teasing. He hadn't forgotten Paige's reaction to his dismissal of the teaching plans she'd first developed for Rosa.

She grinned at him and he let out the breath he hadn't realised he was holding. After last night, he wanted them to be relaxed around each other, but he'd needed to make sure. She'd melted in his arms, under his tongue, but until now he'd had no guarantee that he hadn't merely been a source of stress relief for her. Whereas for him…

"I do." His heart leapt at her words – a thoughtless turn of phrase, no doubt – as she stepped around his desk and presented him with a scroll of paper. "Rosa would like to extend an invitation to dinner tonight."

Mareko accepted her offering without speaking. He could claim that he had dinner with Rosa every night, but they'd both know he was lying. Since taking on the additional marketing role, he'd been in the office until the sun dipped below the horizon more nights than not.

Unrolling the paper, he saw 'Menu' printed at the top in Samoan, followed by a list of his favourite foods. Oka and keke pua'a, with paifala to finish. At the bottom, a note - dinner would be served at seven sharp.

A smile tugged at his lips. "Is she making all of this herself?"

"I'm helping," Paige admitted. "But it was Rosa's idea. She planned the menu and we've already been to the market to choose the fish for the oka. She wanted it as fresh as possible. I think she may have hustled the fishmonger actually, but I can't be sure."

A laugh burst out of Mareko. "That does sound like her." Glancing up, he took in Paige's surprised expression. "What is it?"

Pink crawled up Paige's neck but she met his eyes steadily. "That's the first time I've heard you laugh," she admitted. "You should do it more. It's lovely."

Mareko stared at her dumbly, the thumping of his heart all he could hear above the ever-present whirr of the resort's air conditioning.

"Oh," he finally managed. "Thank you."

Paige nodded, her cheeks still flushed. They stared at each other, eyes locked, and Mareko's stomach tightened. Whatever was happening here, it was significant. More so than when he'd met Hélène, even. Hélène had been magnificent, and he'd been in awe of her. Vibrant and passionate - the kind of passion that peaked and troughed regularly, meaning he never knew what version of his late wife he would be returning home to. But in the wake of Hélène's revelation that she never loved him and with several years in his rearview mirror, he had no illusions as to the reality of their relationship. If not for Rosa, their desire would have died a natural death and they would have parted ways as friends and colleagues. This... thing... this uncomfortable prickle under the surface of his skin when he thought of Paige, the flare of heat in his chest when her green eyes met his... it hinted at something bigger than a holiday fling and a few recreational bedroom activities.

The thought was sobering. Paige was here for two weeks more at most. She had a job – a life – in New Zealand. As for him, his life was here. The Moananui. His daughter and his parents and his employees. They depended on him. The last thing he needed was to be distracted by unruly feelings he couldn't decipher and the inevitable trainwreck that would follow should he decide to act on them.

Clearing his throat, he broke eye contact with Paige and glanced back down at the paper he held in his hands.

"Unfortunately, I don't know if I can make it. I have a conference call at six-thirty that might run late."

He heard Paige swallow but he didn't look up, instead focusing on the careful swoops of his daughter's handwriting. That was where he needed to be focusing his attention. On the world he lived in, the people who relied on him. Emotions were messy, complicated, devious. They could fool a man into believing lust was love and passion was compatibility. Business was precise, measurable. The black figures in his spreadsheet would be the proof of his love for his family, and that was what mattered. Not this temporary hunger that chewed at him and whispered untenable thoughts in his ear. Thoughts like *what if…*

"Mareko?"

"Yes?"

"Have dinner with your daughter."

He looked up then. Paige's bottom lip was caught between her teeth, her green eyes pleading.

"She loves you so much," she continued when he didn't respond. "You told me once that Rosa just wanted to spend time with me, enjoy my company. Well, that's even truer of you. I know what you do in this office is important to you, but what's important to her is that she sees you, talks to you." A shadow passed across her face. "Trust me, all kids really want is to know their parents are interested in them as people. She's gone to a great deal of trouble for this meal, for no reason other than the fact that she thinks it will make you happy. Make her happy and accept."

Mareko swallowed past the lump in his throat. She was right. Of course she was right. She was beautiful, brilliant, and entirely correct.

"Please tell Rosa I would be honoured to attend her dinner."

"She does require a formal RSVP," the woman who had confounded his logical mind with a single compliment about his laugh prodded. "There's a card on the back to respond."

"Ah." Mareko located the card, registering his acceptance quickly with the fountain pen he kept on his desk specifically for contract signings, and held it out towards Paige without meeting her eyes. Instead, he stared at the aqua chairs in front of his desk.

*Perhaps after we see an increased turnover they could be recovered. Maybe a deeper blue. Rosa could help pick out the colour.* The thought distracted him almost enough that he didn't notice when Paige slipped the reply card from his fingers and quietly disappeared from his office.

He sent an email rescheduling the conference call, set an alarm on his phone for six forty-five and threw himself back into his work. The scheduled posts across social media were generating more positive feedback than the resort had seen since news of the *One True Love* finale mishap had spread, but he suspected more organic growth would be possible through promoting the wild beauty of Samoa as a whole. He made a note to contact local photographers to discuss partnership opportunities as well as capturing unstaged shots of his own.

In the afternoon, he collected his mother and Rosa from the bungalow and drove them to the hospital, where his father seemed to be recuperating well. They stayed for an hour, Rosa eating the pudding cup her grandfather had saved her from his lunch tray and filling him in on resort gossip, while Mareko tracked down his doctor and made copious notes during their conversation that he could decipher at home with Paige.

"How is your nanny working out for you?" Enele enquired when he returned to the room.

Speak of the angel...

"She's good," Mareko replied, keeping his eyes on his phone. His father had always had an uncanny knack for reading his emotions – one of the reasons he hadn't wanted to move back to the island with Hélène. "She's been very helpful with Rosa."

"I can make macarons now," Rosa supplied, licking the last traces of chocolate pudding off her spoon.

"You can?" Enele was clearly impressed. "Such a clever girl."

Rosa's chest puffed out with pride. "*And* paifala. Including the pastry!"

"You are a marvel. What else has your nanny been teaching you?"

Mareko half listened as his daughter rattled off her new learning in emergency first aid and budgeting. "I've been teaching Paige some Samoan, and the sasa as well," Rosa continued, referring to one of the island's more popular dances. The fact that it could be performed in a seated position meant it was often the first one taught to children – a starter to the use of dance as a way of celebrating that would stick with every Samoan child for life. Even though he'd lived overseas for years, the impulse to move his hips, his feet in the intricate patterns of his childhood every time he heard the strike of wood on wood from a Pasifika drum never failed. It was part of him, entwined so deeply in his identity, in his very soul, that he knew he would never be free of it. Not that he wanted to.

*Fa'a Samoa. The Samoan way.*

The idea of Paige learning his language, his culture, even for her brief stay, tugged at his stomach.

Enele's eyebrows raised. "Really? Your palagi nanny knows the sasa?"

"She's not that good at it," Rosa conceded, her nose wrinkling. "But I can tell she's trying hard. And she tells me that trying our best is the most important thing, whether we succeed or not."

Mareko snorted softly at that. It was a lovely sentiment for Paige to inspire in his daughter, but all previous encounters with his nanny indicated that Paige put a high premium on success for herself.

They finished up their visit soon after – the doctor had encouraged Mareko not to overstimulate Enele during the first few days of his recovery and the endless chatter from both Mareko's mother and daughter was enough stimulation for anyone in small doses. As they began filing out of the room though, Enele motioned Mareko over to his bedside with a jerk of his head.

"Tama?"

"Your nanny," Enele intoned, his watery brown eyes steady on Mareko.

"What about her?"

"She's the one."

His father's meaning took a moment to register. *The one what?* The one that drove him crazy, with her peach scent and tiny yellow bikini? The one that looked after his child, with endless patience and a logical approach to achieving goals? The one from the television show, where she'd been cast as the airheaded girl next door, stumbling into date after date with the slimy Patrick?

So Mareko had streamed a couple of episodes. Sue him.

Then Enele's hand gripped his, huge and calloused, and Mareko returned his attention to his face.

"She's the one," his father repeated.

"For what?" *Don't say it, don't say it.*

"For you."

"Tama." Mareko couldn't bring himself to shake off his father's hand, but he squeezed it as he forced out a laugh. "You met her for the first time last night."

"It doesn't matter," Enele insisted. "I knew when I saw the two of you together."

"You'd just come out of surgery. You had more drugs in your system than a Rolling Stone."

Enele shook his head stubbornly. "I know what I saw. And Rosa says she's learning the language, the sasa? Mark my words, boy. That girl is the one for you."

Mareko turned his father's assurances over in his head all the way home. Paige was lovely, no doubt. Even discounting her gorgeous face and luscious body. But he'd never bought into the idea of 'the one'. The world was too vast, full of too many people, to believe that there could be one person out there meant for everyone. The chances of meeting them out of all the billions of people in the world were impossibly slim. Not to mention the fact that he didn't have time for a relationship. Paige herself had pointed out how thinly he was stretched. He had his priorities, his family and the resort. And soon, Paige would return to her own life – to New Zealand and her role as a doctor, a role she'd spent years preparing for. There was no future for them. She was indulging in a holiday fling, and he was happy to help. He'd fought it, fought against the lust that shadowed his every interaction with her, trying hard to remain professional. He'd lost that battle, but that was a battle of the flesh. Desire, as dark as it could be, was not dangerous. Love? Love could ruin a man. Love could ruin families. The illusion of it had already destroyed his own family once. He would never put himself in that position again.

*No*, he reasoned, as he pulled the van in behind the bungalow, Penina and Rosa disembarking and scurrying into the house while he climbed out and continued down the path towards his office. *Tama is imagining things.*

But when he entered the bungalow precisely at seven pm that night and saw Paige standing next to a proud Rosa, candlelight painting her skin pink and gold, all of his favourite foods laid out on a starched white tablecloth next to gleaming silver cutlery, his heart skipped a beat.

*Well*, Mareko thought, as Rosa darted forward to pull his chair out for him. *That's inconvenient.*

Rosa was a culinary genius.

The oka was delicious – chunks of raw fish marinated in coconut cream with tomato, cucumber and a squeeze of citrus – blowing every ceviche dish Paige had ever tried out of the water. It was followed by steamed pork buns, completely handmade by Rosa. Paige hadn't been allowed near the dough after the struggle she'd had making panipopo the night before. In fact, the sticky mass she'd been fighting to knead into a workable dough before the call about Enele's health had still been on the kitchen counter this morning when she woke. She'd cleaned it all away, dumping the dough in the rubbish and scrubbing the kitchen til it gleamed. Part of her efforts were an attempt to reduce as much of Penina's stress as possible, but a sliver gave her the opportunity to examine the previous night's events in detail, rolling them around in her mind and examining them from each angle as she worked. Busy hands, busy brain. And last night had given her plenty to concentrate on. The hospital. The phone call with her mother. Mareko, comforting her... cradling her... making her lose all control as he stared down at her from where he lay nestled between her thighs, the low light of her bedside lamp glowing golden in his dark hair.

"Paige?"

She jumped, startled at the sound of her name. Heat rose in her cheeks as she realised Rosa, Mareko and Penina were all watching her.

"Pardon? I was distracted." *Distracted thinking about the best sex of my life.*

And wasn't that the most tragic part? Years occasionally dating trained medical professionals and a former fiancé in her past, and the most titillating sexual experience she'd had was with her temporary employer who made a habit of avoiding her whenever possible. Not only that, he'd found her clitoris with more speed and accuracy than any future doctor she'd dated before. Perhaps she needed to contact the Medical Council about making it part of the final exams. Letting cishet male doctors out into the world when they couldn't even identify basic body parts seemed like a violation of her Hippocratic oath. Certainly it violated her own personal principles about helping other women. There was no way having their labia lips frantically dry-rubbed by someone who was supposed to have professional working knowledge of anatomy was in anyone's best interests.

"I asked if you wanted a pineapple pie?" Rosa held up the platter of rustic handmade pies, dusted with icing sugar. "They're Papa's favourite."

"I'd love one, thank you." Paige accepted her dessert with a smile. Rosa had outdone herself. While Paige harboured her own reservations about the girl's motivation for mastering the art of pastry, she certainly had talent to match her determination. And if there was one thing Paige appreciated even more than hard work, it was dessert.

She bit into her pie, the sweet tartness of the pineapple filling exploding in her mouth.

*Delicious.*

Looking up, she caught Mareko's gaze. Everything tightened in her, awareness buzzing across her skin like electricity. His dark eyes remained locked on hers, sliding away to focus on her mouth when she licked her lips free of powdered sugar. A muscle ticked in his jaw and Paige squeezed her legs together.

"You're enjoying it?" His voice was a deep rumble across the table, molten chocolate that licked across her skin.

"Yes." Surely that couldn't be her own voice? Surely Paige had never sounded so delicate, so... wispy? Swallowing, she tried again. "You have excellent taste."

Hunger flared in Mareko's gaze that had nothing to do with dessert. "I'm glad you think so."

Holy crap, those eyes! The way he looked at her, taking in every detail of her face and moving lower, his gaze caressing her neck, her shoulders, her breasts...

It was knowing.

It was intimate.

It was... the most aroused she'd ever been.

How he could make her this way, anticipation flooding her veins, like there was an arrow dipped in desire at her throat and a single prick, a single word, a single movement from him would send her spiralling into an unknown heat was a mystery Paige had no intention of solving. In the back of her mind she was aware of finishing her pastry, Rosa and Penina leaving the table with talk of an evening swim, but all of her focus was on Mareko.

Mareko, with his tie loose, his shirtsleeves rolled up to reveal strong, brown forearms.

Mareko, who held her gaze as he sipped his water, condensation trickling down the side of the glass to pool against his strong fingers.

Mareko, leaning forward, swallowing hard.

Rosa and Penina called out their goodbyes, the slamming of the screen door behind them punctuating their departure. And in the loaded silence left in their wake, Mareko's accented voice rolling over her body like a physical caress, his whispers branded on her skin, leaving gooseflesh in their wake.

"Tell me, Paige Beckett. Since we are now all alone here, what shall we do?"

They barely made it to her bedroom.

Afterwards, Paige lay sated in his arms, her head pressed to the muscular planes of his chest. The thu-thump of Mareko's heart echoed her own as their breathing slowed. This had always been her favourite part of sex. Orgasms were great – she was a big fan – but these long golden moments that stretched between lovers when the act was complete, the sense of connection that came in the wake of sharing bodies and kisses and the vulnerabilities inherent in lovemaking were incomparable. For a girl who was self-aware enough to know that what she truly craved was unconditional love, these stolen moments of connection were almost enough.

It was one of the reasons she'd been careful to avoid casual sex in the past. Paige was all for people having sex with whomever they wanted, as often as they liked and in as many positions and locations as possible. If it was legal and consensual, she was for it. Theoretically, of course. But she knew herself, and the risk of developing romantic feelings for her sexual partners had prevented her from engaging in one-night-stands or flings until this point. Something about the island, about the freedom of knowing nobody outside the resort, had her throwing her usual carnal caution to the wind.

*Or perhaps*, a small voice whispered inside, *it's Mareko*.

Paige shook her head slightly, banishing the voice. She was attracted to Mareko, sure. She suspected ninety-eight percent of straight adult women were. The dichotomy of ruthless businessman in starched shirts and indulgent family man, caring for his ageing parents and twirling his daughter around the living room to Swedish seventies pop music was a dual-sided temptation anyone in her position would be hard-pressed to resist.

And Paige... Well, Paige had never been particularly good at resistance. It had come easy to her throughout her high-school years - weighing up the possibility of disappointing her parents, of causing them yet more worry had won out over any potential peer pressure to drink too heavily or try drugs. Her studious nature had meant that she was oblivious to any romantic overtures, though a couple of boys from school –well, men now, she supposed – had messaged her throughout the screening of *One True Love* to tell her how much they'd liked her during that time. Her former study partner, Erin, had too, which was surprising. Erin was now a bigwig civil engineer in Copenhagen, but she'd apparently been kept up to date on Paige's *One True Love* journey through her mother and the glory of the Internet. A pity, Paige had mused, when she'd received Erin's message. They could have had a lot more fun at the school dances they'd attended together if Paige had been less oblivious. Nevertheless, they'd made plans to catch up for coffee as friends when Erin was home at Christmas. She'd ignored the messages from her male schoolmates entirely, especially after one of them had decided his poetic missives weren't convincing enough to fully convey his feelings towards her. He'd followed up with picture proof of his 'attraction' and Paige had promptly removed the open messaging feature of her app and diverted all unknown senders to her junk folder.

So no, she hadn't been called on much in her life to resist temptation. And the enthusiasm and, frankly, athleticism she'd just displayed with Mareko indicated that her resistance towards the tall, dark resort owner in particular was about as effective as custard resisting a sword.

"What are you thinking about?" Mareko's voice, gravelly with satisfaction broke her reverie. One large hand skimmed up her naked back and back down, alighting nerve endings she'd thought might have perished in the wake of her explosive orgasm.

"Custard," she replied, because it was poor form to let your casual bed partner know you were falling madly for them. "You?"

He huffed out a laugh, his breath warm against her hair. "The resort."

"Always the resort, huh?" Her voice was light, teasing, but his was not when he replied.

"Always."

Paige pushed herself up slightly to meet his eyes. "It weighs on you that badly?"

A soft smile tugged at the corners of Mareko's mouth, and he reached out to tuck a swath of hair behind her ear.

"Quite the opposite. It is an honour to be able to carry on the work my grandparents started, to work to leave Rosa a legacy she can inherit. It is not easy," he sighed, leaning back and looking up at the ceiling, "but it is a weight I was born to bear."

"You don't want to do anything else?"

Mareko was silent for a long moment. Just when she'd thought he wasn't going to answer, he spoke, his voice quiet. "I always wanted to work in the industry, but when I was younger I thought I wanted to do so elsewhere. Samoa is a small country, and I had dreams of seeing the world. So I did. I studied in London and Paris. I worked in Cairo. Before Rosa was born I took time off, holidays, flitted around here and there and lived the life of a twenty-something without responsibility."

"You didn't enjoy it?"

A slight head shake. "I forgot who I was. I forgot my responsibilities." His voice grew hard. "My parents wanted to retire, but I was in line for a big promotion in Cairo. The resort was amazing, the pay astronomical. It was obvious Hélène wasn't happy in our relationship by then, and she'd been very clear that she didn't want to move to a tiny island in the middle of the Pacific, miles from her family and friends in France. So I spoke to my tina and tama, explained that I couldn't come home and take over The Moananui. I told them I'd sort everything out, ensure they didn't have to put their retirement on hold for me."

"That sounds like a reasonable solution," Paige offered. She rested her chin against Mareko's pectoral muscle in time to feel the snort roll through him.

"I hired a general manager to run the resort for them. All the applications came through me, I did the interviewing. I hired a man called Edwin Glass. He had exceptional references, and was coming off a job as Chief Financial Officer for a resort in Malaysia."

"What happened?" Paige breathed. There was more to this story. She could tell by the set of his jaw.

"He was an embezzler. Tens of thousands of dollars he skimmed from The Moananui. From my people, from my *family*," Mareko's voice was thick with anger. "We were on the verge of financial ruin when I moved home and discovered his betrayal. We're still not back to the level of financial security we were when my father was in charge, before I let my selfish desires overrule my responsibilities."

"You couldn't have known." Paige tried to comfort him, but Mareko shook his head.

"I should have known," he argued. "I should have checked his references more carefully – he falsified them, of course. I should have come back and checked on the resort, on my parents, more. I didn't return until two years later, after Hélène died. I was afraid of them seeing us together, to be honest. I knew my parents would be able to see that we weren't in love and I couldn't stand disappointing them. Not after I'd already broken their hearts by eloping to Lyon. In the end, my shame cemented their strife. If I had swallowed my pride, come home sooner... I might have seen what he was doing. I could have stopped it."

"Oh, Mareko." Paige reached up and cupped his cheek. Her heart ached for him, for the pressure and guilt this beautiful man carried around in him under pressed cotton and a granite demeanour. "It's not your fault. Nobody saw it. How long were you back when you discovered the embezzlement?"

"He was arrested two weeks after I returned."

"See? People were here for two years and didn't notice. You acted as soon as you found out. Your parents are some of the loveliest people I've ever met. I'm sure they don't blame you for what happened."

Mareko captured the hand on his cheek and dragged it across his stubbled jaw, pressing a kiss to her palm.

"Perhaps they don't," he admitted softly. "But I do. Until the day I leave this earth, everything I do will be to make amends to them. I know you think I work too hard, that I need to spend more time with Rosa. You're probably right, to be honest. But all the work I do is for her. For her future. My family and this resort's success are the only things that matter."

# CHAPTER 8

"*A* stomach flu?"

Rachel bit her lip. "I'm afraid so."

Mareko let out a soft curse and sat back in his ergonomic chair. "This can't come at a worse time."

Tonight was the first Wednesday fiafia night, and Rachel's prediction had proven correct – the event was fully booked. Several private accommodation vendors had been in touch to thank the resort for providing a mid-week show that they could recommend to guests, and to organise transport to and from The Moananui.

"How many of the dancers has it affected?"

Rachel checked the tablet in her hand. "We're missing two women and three men for tonight, even after some of next week's dancers volunteered to come in and cover."

Mareko nodded, his mind whirring. "Alright. That keeps the female performance in the odd numbers still, so they can adapt the dances from five to three by taking out the back line. But we need at least five for the male performance or the choreography will be unsalvageable."

"I asked around the employees and nobody else was confident enough with the steps." Rachel hesitated. "There is one option."

"Anything." There was no way he could afford for this venture to fail. It needed to be a rousing success, to prove to the other resorts that despite their setbacks The Moananui still had what it took to lead the way in luxury Samoan accommodation.

"You could do it."

Mareko blinked slowly. Twice. He must have misheard. "Pardon me?"

"You were part of the performance group in high school."

"High school was a very long time ago, Rachel." He was thirty-one, for heavens' sake. No matter how hard he worked in the resort gym each morning, he was unprepared for a forty-five minute Pasifika dance routine.

"You know the dances, Mareko," Rachel pointed out. "In fact, you're the one who taught them to Loto when he came on board as the dance leader. And since Loto is currently curled up in the foetal position next to a bucket, you're our only option."

Mareko searched his mind for an alternative but, as usual, Rachel was right. Splitting the dance troupe into two hadn't accounted for what a wave of sickness might do if nobody else was available to cover.

*Fuck.*

"Fine," he groused. "But I need a refresher. Can you please have Sione meet me at my place in an hour to go over the routines with me? And while we're doing that, gauge the interest of other staff members in learning the routines and being available on-call as replacements in the future? We'll need more people comfortable with filling in now that we're doing two shows a week."

Rachel tapped away on her tablet as he spoke, and not for the first time, Mareko was struck with admiration for how efficiently she took care of things. His parents had made an excellent decision in hiring her as a cleaner out of high school. She'd excelled in that role, as she'd gone on to excel in every role she'd had at The Moananui since, jumping from promotion to promotion in the last decade or so, even once the demands of balancing parenting with work had begun.

"Will do," she said, finishing her notes and tucking the tablet under her arm. "I'll also rustle up a spare performance lavalava and have it sent over. You have your own ula nifo?"

"Yes." Mareko had used the same traditional necklace for years. Designed with long ivory resin curves designed to simulate the whale teeth his ancestors had collected, interspersed with dark brown kukui nut beads, his ula nifo had been handmade by his grandmother and presented to him upon his high school graduation. He would wear it until it fell apart.

"And you don't need your chest waxed?"

Mareko closed his eyes and prayed for patience. And pain tolerance, because, yes, in fact, he would need his chest waxed. And that shit *hurt*.

"I'll head to the spa. Thank you for your help," he added as Rachel moved towards the door, and she waved in acknowledgment as she exited as though it was nothing.

It did not seem like nothing an hour later when Rosa laughed so hard that she fell off the couch at his announcement that he would miss dinner that night as he would be performing in the fiafia celebration.

"Can you even dance?" she managed through peals of laughter.

Mareko feigned affront, but his mother's was real. "Your father is one of the best dancers I have ever seen," she scolded her granddaughter. "He moves like the river flows."

Mareko's cheeks heated until they were almost as pink as his post-waxed pecs at her obvious lie, as he met Paige's eyes over Penina's head.

"Like the river flows?" she mouthed at him, and the amusement on her face caused him to grin.

"Like a river," he mouthed back, tilting his head arrogantly and her own grin split her heart-shaped face.

"This I have to see," Paige announced at normal volume. "How do I book a ticket?"

"I don't think watching Dad prance half naked around the stage is worth your hard-earned money," Rosa informed her even as a giggle burst forth from her lips. "Employees can go free as long as you sit at the back."

"Half-naked, you say?" Paige pulled a face at Rosa. "Yuck." But her eyes lit on Mareko, taking stock of him in a lengthy perusal that stirred his blood. She was playing with fire, flirting in front of his family, but he couldn't deny he loved the bite of danger it brought. For a second he let himself imagine what would happen if they were alone right now. He'd pull her to him, press her up against where he was hard and aching, and prove he had moves. Not stage-appropriate moves, perhaps, but moves nonetheless.

He couldn't ever remember wanting a woman this way. It wasn't only her body either, wonderland that it was. It was her soul. He didn't have to look any further than the way she'd been accepted with open arms by his family and the rest of the resort staff to see how her kindness and empathy drew people in. And the way she'd comforted him after his father's heart attack? Paige Beckett was an extraordinary woman. If she was staying any longer than the month he would be at serious risk of losing his head over her. Maybe even his heart.

It was better for everyone that their time together was limited, Mareko decided, even as he let his gaze linger on the soft swell of her breasts beneath the thin tank top she wore. When their time was up, they could part on friendly terms, each carrying fond memories of a beautiful fling together. There would be none of the messy devolution that hallmarked longer relationships. He wouldn't feel the sharp press of familial duty between his shoulder blades, competing with the woman standing in front of him and her desires. Who knows? Maybe she'd come back to visit one day, and they'd share a cocktail and reminisce over the weeks they spent together in the wake of a wedding scandal.

"Boss?" Sione rapped on the frame of the open bungalow door. "Are you ready?"

Mareko shook his head, returning his focus to the present. There would be no resort for Paige to return to if he couldn't salvage it. The additional fiafia nights were a solid strategy for generating consistent income that could be used to support his staff and their families, while maintaining and upgrading the facilities. That needed to be his focus. Not a platinum blonde with rosebud lips and a laugh that rang like music through the rafters of his home.

"Ready as I can be with such short notice," he responded evenly, and Sione grinned at him. Mareko knew that the extra money the bartender earned as one of the fiafia dancers went directly into a university fund for his children. Mareko couldn't risk messing this up.

"We'll get out of your way, let you practice." Paige

gathered up her things, motioning to Rosa. Mareko flashed her a grateful smile. She'd read his mind.

"I'll see you at the fiafia night." She shot him a cheeky grin and Mareko heard Sione laugh low behind him.

"Something funny?" he asked as Paige and Rosa hustled out of the door and Penina retired to her room with her bag of crochet yarn.

"No, boss," Sione smirked. "This is going to be good, that's all."

"What do you mean?"

"You'll see. Now, loosen those hips, boss man. Let's see what you've got."

THE FIAFIA NIGHT was underway when Paige made her way into the large fale that hosted the performances. Rosa had told her that afternoon that during the rainy season the celebration was held in the resort's Hibiscus Room; but the majority of the year when the weather was fine it took place outdoors within the simple open-air structure, a domed roof thatched with dried sugarcane leaves providing shade and cover for guests.

Long tables filled the centre of the room, dressed in white linen and shiny silver utensils. There was no assigned seating for ticket holders apparently, the very design of the tables encouraged a sense of community, sharing food and conversation. At one end of the room, a veritable feast was laid out buffet-style. Full roasted pigs presided over a delicious smelling array of traditional Polynesian foods, along with salads, breads and a seafood station that would be more familiar to international guests. Once more, Paige marvelled at how well The Moananui walked the line between a cultural experience and comfortable surroundings for its guests. There was the opportunity for visitors to immerse themselves almost fully in island life through adventure and agricultural tourism packages, or to simply laze by the pool and soak up the tropical environment with all the luxuries of home.

At the other end of the room from the feast was a low, rectangular stage. A Western-style drum kit sat at the back along with a Pasifika drum station, the cylindrical wooden drums fashioned from tree branches and carved with traditional patterns representing the land and important customs of the island propped on special stands that held them above the ground. Paige had seen them in use at the market when she and Paige visited and the myriad of sounds such a simple instrument could produce depending on where it was struck and the talent of the musician had amazed her.

"Paige!" A young woman she recognised as one of the kitchen staff waved her over to the buffet. "Sau! Come, grab a plate before the show begins."

Paige loaded her plate with a range of delicacies and headed to the round table to the back left of the room that the woman indicated was for staff. There was nobody else there when she took a seat though – the stomach virus that had wiped out members of the performance troupe was clearly effective.

She'd just taken her first bite, savouring the flavours of coconut and taro leaves, when a drumbeat reached the exposed rafters.

*Ba-da-dum.*

*Ba-da-dum. Ba-da-dum.*

*Ba-da-dum. Ba-da-dum. Ba-da-dum.*

"Chee-hoo!" A male voice filled the space, pulling

diners' attention from their plates and towards the stage as five men filed out. They were all wearing matching purple lavalavas and necklaces that seemed to be made of beads and bone, but Paige only had eyes for Mareko. He stood at the end of the row, hands behind his back, eyes fixed straight ahead. His short black hair was brushed back from his face and shone under the simple stage lights. His chest was broad, looking for every inch like he spent his days working the land or collecting bounty from the sea rather than sitting behind a desk. His muscles gleamed with oil, smooth save the dark treasure trail Paige was intimately familiar with leading from his taut stomach down, bisecting the muscled V of his hips, before dipping beneath the thin cotton that wrapped around them.

Desire swirled and knotted her stomach. He looked like raw masculinity, like power and sex and safety, all wrapped up in smooth brown skin and topped with a face that would make angels weep.

And he was hers.

Not forever, of course. She had responsibilities she needed to get back to her, as much as the thought sat like lead in her abdomen. But for now... for now she could sit back and enjoy delicious food and take in the form and lines of the man she was lucky enough to share a bed with.

And then he started to dance.

There was nothing else after that. No food, no guests, no other dancers. There was only Mareko, stomping, clapping, swirling his hips. He threw his head back, grinning widely, the column of his throat working under the lights as he cried out his joy and pride. His feet were wide apart, knees bent, and the gyration of his body should have made Paige blush, but she was too busy appreciating it.

She crossed her legs and squeezed her thighs together as

the rhythm of the drums pounded the air, keeping time with the throb of lust that pulsed at her centre. Mareko was a dynamo in well-tailored suits, but this was something else. Unfiltered sensuality rolled off him, and with every slap of his palms against his powerful thighs, every undulation of his thickly muscled body, Paige's need grew.

The music changed, the frenzy of drums slowing to a heavier, dirtier beat as Mareko took centre stage. He was a force of nature, the stress he'd worn like a suit since she met him gone. Instead, his movements were loose and easy as he led the men through a series of suggestive movements, his skin glowing like burnished gold under the lights, hips snapping back and forth as he smiled out towards his audience.

Then his eyes landed on Paige and darkened, the smile fading from his face until only intensity remained. There was no laughter now, none of the easy flirtation that had peppered the earlier dance. This was different. *She* was different, because when he looked at her with that heat in his eyes, moving his body across that stage like he did in bed, she was overcome with the need to drag him off the platform and into a dark corner. For a woman who'd spent her life trying to please everyone else, she was suddenly desperate to give in to the selfish drive that threatened nothing but carnal pleasure.

*I want him.*

He could feel it too, she could tell by his expression. Lust drew itself in stark relief across his face, from the tightness in his jaw to the colour that flushed his high cheekbones.

*Mana.* She'd heard the concept before, but now she saw it. Authority. Power. The divine, elemental drive embodied in human form. That was how Mareko felt to her right now. That was how he made *Paige* feel. Like she wasn't confined to skin and bone, but instead made up of stars and dust, of *feeling*. Their connection stretched across the room, an invisible thread as delicate as a spiderweb but as strong as gold. Unbreakable.

Paige barely noticed when the music stopped, her eyes locked on Mareko. He didn't follow the other performers off the stage, instead he hopped directly off the stage and strode through the room, his gaze unwavering on her.

Anticipation wrenched tighter in her, hardening her nipples at his approach. He didn't speak, merely held out his hand. She took it, letting him pull her out of her chair, as powerless to deny him as she was to stop a hurricane. She didn't *want* to deny him, she admitted to herself as he led her out of the fale and through the night towards the bungalow. More than that, she didn't want to deny herself. She was here for such a limited time, free from the watchful gaze of her parents, her mentor in her GP registrar programme, the soulless lens of the camera. Finally, there was nobody watching her, judging her for trying to find some pleasure where she could. Whatever this was, this pull, Paige was done holding back. She followed Mareko up the stairs of their shared home, let him tug her into her bedroom, closing the door behind them without a word. He kissed her, hot and hungry, and she kissed him back, her hands roaming over the smooth skin of his back, tracing his hips, revelling in the luxury of having this man all to herself. Her fingers tugged at the knot holding the flimsy cloth around his waist and he moved to help her, the fabric falling to the floor beneath their feet. Paige reached into his underwear and wrapped her hand around his thick cock, stroking it the way she knew now he liked – tight at the base, working her thumb lightly over the tip when she reached it.

"Paige. *Fuck.*" Mareko growled the broken words into the

air and she shushed him with a smothered laugh before Rosa or Penina could hear. He shucked his briefs and fell backwards onto the bed, his cock standing at attention, eyes intent on her as she unbuttoned the front of her sundress, teasing him with the sliver of skin that peeked out as each new button loosened.

"Finally," he murmured as she slipped the straps off her shoulders and let it pool on the polished floorboards, leaving her in nothing but her lace underwear. "Get over here."

She moved towards him, but when he held out his arms for her, she shook her head.

"You were amazing tonight," she said, guiding his arms back down to the cream coverlet and crawling up the bed to nuzzle his jaw. Mareko sighed, tilting his head so she could kiss the place where his neck met his shoulder.

"I am glad you liked it, lo'u alofa." His voice was husky and Paige shivered, desire and anticipation thrumming in her blood.

"I loved it," she whispered. "They way you moved…It reminded me of sex."

Mareko let out a hoarse laugh. "Everything about you reminds me of sex."

"You are so full of crap."

"Honestly," he claimed, catching her hips and settling her over him until she straddled his lap. Paige let herself sink down, let the warm head of his cock press against her through the soft lace, working herself in small movements as the fabric built friction against her most sensitive area. "Every time I see you in that bikini, I want to pull the cups aside and suck your pretty nipples into my mouth. When you're laughing with someone else, I imagine you smiling up at me from your knees with my cock in your mouth. That little moan you make when you eat?" He groaned. "It sounds just like the one you make when I sink inside you. Everything you do drives me crazy. It doesn't matter how many times I've had you, I'm constantly aching for my next chance."

Pleasure rose in Paige as he spoke, the picture he painted of a temptress so at odds with the way she saw herself.

"Do you like that?" she asked, her voice shy even as she rocked her hips harder, pressing down against the thick ridge between her legs.

"I fucking love it," Mareko growled. "Does it make you feel good? Knowing you have me so twisted in knots I can't sit through the workday without wanting to race home and bury myself in you?"

"Yes," she admitted, rocking harder now.

"Good." Mareko said, one hand fumbling in her bedside drawer. He handed her a condom from the box they'd stashed there the first night. "Now stop playing around and put me in. I've been hard for you since I saw you sitting there watching me dance. You're lucky I didn't poke someone's eye out with my erection."

Paige smirked, but lifted herself onto her knees, sliding the fabric of her underwear to the side and rolled the latex down his shaft. He was thick and dark, the full mushroom tip flush with blood, and she squeezed his balls as she positioned herself.

Mareko sucked in a breath, lifting his head to watch as she notched him at her entrance and rolled her hips down, taking every inch of him.

"Beautiful," he whispered, eyes locked on the spot where their bodies joined, and Paige pressed down that little bit further, a tiny moan escaping as the thick thatch of Mareko's curls brushed over her clit.

"That's it. That's my girl. Give me that little extra, huh? What an overachiever." She could hear the smile in Mareko's voice and she shot him one of her own, pleasure pressing in against her from all sides. He was deeper than he'd ever been in this position, and she relished it, the warm stretch of her body accommodating him, welcoming the invasion, and the power she held perched on top of him like a queen.

She moved then, a slow ride, her hips moving, spinning magic into the air that sizzled between them. Mareko held himself still under her as she picked up speed, tucking her feet under the heavy weight of his hair-dusted thighs for momentum. Keeping his eyes on hers, he reached up to toy with one of her nipples. Paige rocked harder, grinding down onto him, the pleasure-pinch of pain shooting down her abdomen, making her wetter. The sound of their lovemaking echoed in the quiet air, punctuated with stifled moans and grunts as Mareko's other hand clasped the flesh of her arse, using it to aid her movements. Paige tipped her head back, luxuriating in the thrill of owning her pleasure, of taking what she needed from the big, strong man between her thighs who was whispering encouragement to her as she rocked herself closer to the edge, telling her how beautiful she was, how hot and tight she was around him, how good she was making him feel. Then his thumb moved to her clit, holding steady as her hips lost their rhythm, uneven slides now up and down the thick column of flesh filling her.

"Paige. Look at me," Mareko commanded quietly, and she did, she opened her eyes and met his dark gaze and that did it, she exploded, her orgasm washing over her like a tsunami while he watched, eyes steady on her as she shuddered and gasped through her climax, and Paige let herself drown.

She slumped forward onto Mareko's chest, breathless, and he banded strong arms behind her back, thrusting up from beneath her as he chased his own pleasure, a long groan wrenching from him as he came up into her, their pants painting the air around them as they held tight to each other in the darkness.

# CHAPTER 9

"Ten thousand," Rosa announced, holding up Paige's phone.

"Ten thousand what?" Paige replied absentmindedly. She was bent in half, searching for her missing flip flop under her bed. Living out of a suitcase was all fine and dandy, except her footwear options were incredibly limited. She'd packed one pair of flip flops, one pair of sneakers, and her wedding sandals. And one of her flip flops appeared to have been casualty to her passionate night with Mareko.

*Not the only casualty.* She could admit privately that there had been a pinch in her chest this morning when she woke and realised he was gone once more. Logically, she understood that it was for the best – it would be a nightmare for Rosa to catch them in bed together or Penina to see him sneaking out of her room. But after last night she could no longer categorise their tryst as a holiday fling. The way Mareko had held her, the beautiful words he'd whispered to her in the dark… she was falling for him. It wasn't smart, as evidenced by her hurt upon waking alone, but it felt inevitable. Like she'd been tumbling towards this since the moment they first locked eyes in the hotel lobby. All she could do was hold on and try to tamp down the whispers in her brain that he was keeping their relationship a secret because he was embarrassed by her, the way Patrick had been.

Mareko was nothing like Patrick, but Paige was still far from trusting her own judgement when it came to men.

"You have ten thousand new followers since you left that slimeball Patrick."

Paige frowned as she moved to sift through her suitcase. "That seems excessive." She wasn't a big social media person at the best of times, but Natalia from *One True Love* had insisted that all contestants set up new accounts to go with their shiny new 'public personas'.

Paige had put about three photos of herself with girls from the show up, a couple of scenery shots, and then promptly forgot about it.

'Oh, hang on, they're newer than that." Rosa's thumbs flew over Paige's screen.

"Come on, Rosa, get off there. You're supposed to be looking up the recipe for tarte tatin." In truth, Paige was a little intimidated by the idea of making their own caramel, but Rosa had pulled her French heritage card, and here they were, about to head off to raid the resort kitchen for supplies.

"Aha!" Scooping up her missing flip flop from the bottom of her suitcase, Paige shoved it onto her foot. Her bright red toenails winked up at her and delight jolted through her as she wiggled them. She'd gone with Rosa and Penina to the spa yesterday and farewelled the pale pink polish she'd been convinced by Natalia was the perfect choice for a soon-to-be bride.

"Paige?"

"Yeah?"

"I think you need to see this." Disquiet swirled in Paige's stomach as she turned to face Rosa. The young girl held her phone out to her. On the screen, Patrick sat frozen, his pretty-boy face set in familiar lines of concern - he'd worn the same expression each week on the show while dismissing the girls he'd declared were not his one true love, one by one.

"I don't want to watch that."

"I think," Rosa's voice was small, "I think he's talking about you."

Paige approached the phone like it was a snarling beast. Taking it from Rosa, she silently pushed the play button and waited as the video for a popular New Zealand current affairs show loaded.

"We're here with Patrick Winslow, star of the *One True Love* reality show, and we hear, a recently jilted groom. How are you, Patrick?"

Her ex-fiancé smiled bravely and Paige barely bit back a groan. Had he always been this bad an actor? "I'm doing well, considering the circumstances, thanks John."

"And what are the circumstances, exactly? We were all under the impression that you and Paige Beckett were flitting off for a tropical island wedding, but here you are alone, without a wedding ring. Can you elaborate for our viewers?"

"I'd be happy to." Patrick took a deep breath. "I was all ready to marry Paige, but she didn't show up. She left a note at the resort desk calling off our wedding without even speaking to me. They told me she'd left minutes before our ceremony was due to begin." He shook his head sadly. "I thought we'd be together forever. She was supposed to be my one true love."

"Were there any signs?" the interviewer probed, and Paige watched Patrick pretend to think.

"I don't want to speak ill of anyone," he lied through his teeth. "But Paige could be quite... juvenile... away from the cameras. She gives off this impression of being sweet and smart and caring, but she sometimes held on to petty things, or threw tantrums when she didn't get her way."

Paige's stomach dropped. "That lying son of a–" she cut herself off when she realised Rosa was studying her intently.

"I don't do that," she assured the younger girl, wracking her brains for any instances Patrick might be referring to. In the short months between the end of the show's filming and their ill-fated wedding, she'd become frustrated with him at times. The egg thing, for sure, though she'd tried to keep that to herself. She'd been more vocal about the wet towels he left all over her flat though, and when he drank all of her flatmate Lily's almond milk without replacing it. But that wasn't juvenile, was it? That was trying to be a responsible adult and a considerate flatmate. In fact, the single time she could really remember having put her foot down was after their engagement party when she'd been trying to get a sloppy Patrick into a taxi and he'd been insistent on going on to drink at some upscale club with his cousins.

She listened a couple of minutes longer as Patrick proceeded to perform a complete hatchet job on her, the dual combination of curiosity and outrage preventing her from stopping the video. And then...

"I think perhaps it's because she had cancer as a child," Patrick mused, and Paige's heart stopped. "Sad, really. But I think for Paige, she's never had to grow up and consider how her behaviour affected others. Someone else always made allowances for her."

Rage blinded Paige as she stabbed at the screen to stop

the video. Anger surged through her blood, electrifying her limbs. Years of conditioning herself to behave appropriately, and the fact that Rosa was watching, stopped her from throwing her phone at the wall. Barely.

*That fucking cockroach. How dare he?*

"Is that true?"

"Is what true?" She snarled up at Mareko, who was leaning against the doorframe, arms crossed. Sometime in the last few seconds she'd slid down off the bed to the polished wooden floor of the bungalow and she let that centre her now, clinging to the cool press of wood against her thighs, trying to bat back the swollen rage that threatened to spill over and consume her.

"Is it true you had cancer as a child?"

She could play it off, tell him it was private medical information, but what was the point? Patrick had already shot the horse of discretion directly in the fucking face.

Instead, she nodded stiffly.

"I'm sorry to hear that." Mareko cleared his throat. "Rosa, would you give Paige and I a minute alone please?"

"Sure." Rosa slid off the bed and padded out of the room on soft feet. Moments later ABBA started playing in the main room, and Paige closed her eyes in silent appreciation for Rosa and her awareness of how sound carried in a space with such high ceilings. The music was Rosa's way of ensuring she and Mareko could speak without being overheard.

A moment later, he settled on the floor next to her, his thigh touching hers.

"Did you know he was doing interviews?"

Paige shook her head. "I should have guessed though. His whole reason for going on the show was to raise his own profile. It's why he picked me over one of the girls he actually liked," she added bitterly. "I should have seen this coming."

She hadn't *wanted* to see it coming. She wanted to sweep the whole messy, humiliating experience away and pretend it had never happened.

Mareko's warm hand settled over hers. "You should never have had to see this coming." He paused. "I take it your health history isn't common knowledge?"

"No," Paige sighed, rolling her head to rest it on one of Mareko's wide shoulders. "I never mentioned it on the show. It's something I told him in confidence, once we were engaged."

"What an arsehole."

Paige huffed out a laugh. "Yeah."

"That's why you don't like hospitals."

"Yeah."

He didn't respond, just rubbed his thumb lightly over the back of her hand.

"How much did you hear?" Paige asked eventually.

"Almost all of it," he admitted. "I was in the living area when it started playing, and, well..."

"The acoustics are not designed for privacy." Paige smiled sadly into his shoulder. "I get it." A beat passed before she couldn't hold it inside any longer. "It didn't make me juvenile, or selfish. The cancer, I mean. It definitely affected me, but not like that. My parents had tried so hard to have me, sacrificed so much. They were so overprotective because of the IVF, because I was their only child. It makes sense of course, and to be honest my mother's worrying is probably the reason I was diagnosed early. But for them to go through all of that to have me, and then for me to be defective–"

"You're not defective," Mareko interrupted fiercely. "You're amazing."

Paige shrugged, even as her chest glowed at his conviction, washing away the worst of the anger that had been simmered under her skin since Patrick's interview.

"That's kind of you to say. But that's not how I felt at the time. I felt like my parents had been given a gift, only to have it turn around and cause problems. *I* felt like a problem. And if they were overprotective before the diagnosis, it was nothing compared to how they behaved afterwards. No contact sports, no processed meats, no parties." She guided his hand further up her arm and pressed his fingers to the scar that ran below her elbow. "I was loved, but I was always aware of how much stress I put my parents under simply by existing. Going on the show was an extension of that. They want grandchildren. I want kids, too. Very much. But more than that, I want them to have what they want. I want them to stop worrying about me, and as sad as it is to admit, a husband and child will help them do that. They'll know I have someone to take care of me if something happens to them. I can take care of myself, but that's not enough for them."

"That's a hard way to live, lo'u alofa."

"Don't misunderstand me, Mareko." Paige lifted her hand from his, but he stayed in place, tracing the dark line of her scar back and forth with a feather-light touch. "I want to get married. I want to have children. Those are my dreams too. I would never do those things simply to assuage my parents' fears. The show seemed like a good way to expedite the process, but my goals haven't changed just because Patrick turned out to be a snake."

"Ioe. Of course." Mareko's voice was soft and she could have sworn he dropped a light kiss against her hair. "I hope you get everything you dream of, Paige. Nobody deserves to find their happy ending more than you. And if you ever want to marry this mysterious future partner of yours at The Moananui, we would be happy to accommodate you."

She burst out laughing at that, joy bubbling out of her. It was astounding, Paige thought, how simply unburdening yourself to someone could relieve tension. She'd never had that before, outside of the therapy programme her training offered in response to the high rates of stress-related leave healthcare professionals required. She'd never brought up the background behind her desire to marry and have children with Patrick, who'd always seemed to assume it was bred into her by virtue of her biology. Certainly, she'd never mentioned to her parents the pressure she felt to provide them with proof she was happy and settled in the form of a family. Preventing them from worrying about her had been Paige's mission in life since the age of nine, and as the *One True Love* debacle had proven, even her attempts to secure a spouse had been fraught with their fears.

"Are you almost done?" Rosa called from outside Paige's bedroom door. "I can hear laughing."

Paige grinned as she untangled herself from Mareko and rose to her feet. "We're done."

"Yippee!" Rosa burst into the room and threw her arms around Paige's middle. "I'm sorry Patrick is such a jerk."

"Me too." Paige hugged her back. "But that's a good lesson to learn, isn't it? Some people will always be jerks, but that doesn't mean we have to give them any power over us. So I say we do something really fun today, so when I look back on this day I'll think about the happiness I had with you, and jerky Patrick won't even cross my mind."

Rosa's eyes lit up. "ABBA impersonator contest?"

Mareko cleared his throat beside them. "As it happens,"

he said, "I've cleared my schedule for the day, and I have something I'd like to do with you."

"Can Paige come?" Rosa demanded.

"Of course," Mareko's smile rose from his daughter's face to include Paige and it was like being enveloped by the sun. "You'll need your bathing suits, though."

Rosa made a face. "It's not the resort pool, is it?"

Mareko's smile grew, flashing his perfect white teeth. "No, afa'fine. It's a little more special than that."

THE PAPASE'EA SLIDING rocks had been a brilliant idea.

He'd brought Rosa before, of course. The naturally formed rock slides, worn smooth from centuries of small waterfalls, were a popular tourist attraction. But it had been at least a year since they'd been.

*Since I took a full day off to spend with her.* The thought painted his insides green with guilt. They'd had days together within that year, but they were holidays more than anything – Easter, Christmas, Samoan Independence Day. And even then, he'd occasionally popped into the office or been called in regarding a resort matter. It had been far too long since he played hooky on a work day and spent it with his daughter. He knew why, hell, even Rosa knew why, but that didn't dismantle the wave of remorse that crept over him as he watched her whoosh down one of the smaller waterfalls on her behind, hands flying up into the air as she dropped towards the crystal clear water below.

*I need to do this more. Before she's too old to even want to spend time with me.*

Rosa's dark head popped out of the water and she tossed

a curtain of wet hair across her shoulder, head tilted back to look up at the waterfall.

"Come on, Paige," she shouted, her voice echoing in the natural hollow of the river. "It's your turn!"

A moment later, Paige flew down the slippery rock, all pale skin and yellow bikini as she hit the water below, a few metres from Rosa. His daughter cheered, and a laugh rumbled out of Mareko. He couldn't remember the last time he'd been this relaxed. Between the resort, his father's health and the pressure of raising Rosa alone, it was very easy to feel like an island himself, awash in a sea of decisions, each one hiding danger in its depths. But today, with the Samoan sun shining down on him, glittering across the water while Rosa and Paige frolicked in the natural pool across from him, warmth spread across his chest. It was contentment, he realised. It had been so long since he'd felt the emotion that it took him longer to recognise than it should have, but the more he turned it over in his head, the surer he was.

He was content. Something about this place, the happiness on his girls' faces, meant he could put aside the burdens he'd been carrying for the last two years. His problems would still be there when he returned to The Moananui, there was no doubt about that, but now, at this moment, they didn't bother him.

He was free.

"Dad!"

A sopping bundle launched herself at him, and he caught her instinctively, burying his nose in her wet hair and inhaling the scent of coconut oil and Rosa.

"Yes, afa'fine?"

"Are you coming in?" Rosa smiled up at him, eyes shining. In moments like this, he could see Hélène in her—

the delicate line of her chin, the sweet curve of her lips. And although she'd left him—left Rosa—in a more permanent way than he would ever have wished on his daughter, he was suddenly grateful for it all. For this moment, which had been set in motion by a thousand moments before it. Moments of ecstasy, and agony, and pride, every one of them leading here, to his daughter wrapped in his arms, smiling up at him on a beautiful day by the water in his homeland.

"Ioe, in a moment," he promised, and she smacked a loud kiss on his cheek.

"I'm going back up for another slide," Rosa hollered towards Paige, levering herself up from his lap and almost making him a eunuch with a misplaced elbow.

"Oof," Mareko grunted, but she was already scampering across the rugged rocks that lined the pool to the bush-lined path that would take her back to the top of the waterfall. It would take her several minutes to get back to the beginning of the gentle rapids but he wasn't worried. Rosa was familiar with the paths and the rains hadn't altered the river's paths since last season. She came here often with Sione's family after church in the hotter months. Yet, as far as he knew, Rosa had yet to discover the sliding rocks' greatest secret.

Sighing, he rose to his feet and headed towards the pool. The water should relieve some of the pain in his groin at least.

"This place is amazing," Paige offered, drifting closer in the water. Mareko gave up on the gentlemanly stance he'd adopted since she whipped off her floaty maxi dress at the water's edge earlier and soaked up the sight of her, lush curves barely contained by flimsy scraps of yellow fabric that made her eyes shine like emeralds and her hair like pewter, slicked back from her face. She was a nymph, a goddess, and he was done pretending that he didn't worship every inch of her.

"You like it?" The water splashed up his calves, rising to his thighs as he waded deeper into the pool. They were lucky to have this smaller pool to themselves—the popularity of the sliding rocks meant they were often packed with tourists as well as locals. Even now, he could hear shrieks of delight from some of the larger pools, where the rocks shot riders out high above the water in exuberant sprays. But here, in this smaller pool, perfect for kids Rosa's age, a canopy of leaves sheltering them, it felt private.

Intimate.

Romantic.

*Perfect.*

Mareko leaned forward into the water, pushing off into a lazy breaststroke. The cool water sluiced off his shoulders but did nothing to dampen the heat coiling beneath his bathing suit.

"I love it," Paige admitted, and his chest hitched at the breathy quality of her voice. Her eyes were fixed on him, his own desire reflected back at him from their green depths and a surge of satisfaction pulsed through him.

*She wants me, too.*

Mareko wasn't used to being undone by a woman. His career had put him in the path of some of the most stunning women the world had seen, but he'd never felt this way before. Even with Hélène, his attraction had flared bright and hot, but it had never held the chord of tenderness that underscored his physical attraction. Perhaps it was the circumstances. Meeting Paige wild-eyed and frantic to flee her wedding had given him a sense of responsibility for her, a degree of caring his past lovers had never managed to secure. Certainly, none of them had made an effort that he could recall. He distinctly remembered Hélène laughing at him once after he'd been affronted on her behalf by a winemaker who had insulted her expertise.

"Calm down, Mareko," she'd drawled, her pouty lips twisted in a way that made him feel she was mocking him. "No woman wants a man ready to throw down gloves for her honour. We want men who will hold out gloves while we fight our own battles."

Be that as it may, Mareko found himself unable to exorcise the vision of Paige fighting back angry tears in her bedroom this morning as she listened to Patrick spill her private medical information over the Internet. The urge to protect her, to take her away from her blasted phone and the devastation it had caused was why they were here now. It was stronger than his admittedly passionate desire to hop a plane to New Zealand and punch a reality TV star in the face. And Mareko had to admit, as he paddled leisurely through the water towards her, that it had been worth it. The worry that had knotted Paige's brows was gone, smoothed away by the joy of the sliding rocks and the healing power of water.

Something about this woman undid him, and while Mareko couldn't put his finger on exactly what it was, he had no qualms in admitting it.

The way her breath caught when he stood, placing a hand on each side of the rocks next to her, hemming her in, was further indication that he was having an impact on her as well.

*Good.*

"I'm pleased you're enjoying yourself, lo'u alofa," he murmured, and Paige's eyes fluttered closed.

"I am. This is just what I needed." Her voice was barely a whisper, yet the pride of providing her with exactly what she desired would have had him beating his chest were it not for a more pressing matter.

"Is there anything else you need?" He trailed his lips over the column of her neck, leaving a trail of gooseflesh in his wake.

Paige whimpered and he adjusted his stance under the water, letting the evidence of *his* need brush against her stomach.

"Mareko." Her eyes flew open, and he lost himself for a moment, dizzy with desire. "We can't. Rosa…"

"Don't worry, lo'u alofa." He brushed his lips against her brow and she sighed, eyes floating shut again. "Sau. Come." Linking their fingers together, he tugged her further into the pool until they floated right by the waterfall. Ducking his head, he swam under the spray, letting the water pummel his back as he kicked through it, coming up in a small cave behind the fall. Paige popped up a moment later, their fingers still entwined.

"Oh, Mareko!" She glanced around, delight etched onto her face. "It's magical."

The cave was tiny compared to some, a simple smooth rock face forming the back wall. The rocks that made up the floor were higher than in the pool proper, meaning the water was waist height when he stood. Light streamed in through the fall of water that concealed the entrance, painting the shadows navy and gold through the spray.

"Yes," Mareko replied, never taking his eyes off Paige. "It's beautiful."

She glanced back at him and flushed, pink creeping up her cheeks as she took him in, standing in the cool blue, hard and aching from wanting her. She must have seen it on his face because her eyes suddenly dropped to where the water lapped at his abdomen – Lord knew, if she could see under water that pink flush would turn beet red in an instant – and when they travelled back up over his chest to meet his, they were firm with determination.

"I really appreciate you taking the time out of your day to bring me here," she said suddenly, and he swallowed hard.

"You're welcome."

"No, I don't think you understand." Eyes still glinting, she moved towards him. When she reached out and trailed a finger down between his pectoral muscles, Mareko almost exploded on the spot. The warmth of her finger was a fiery contrast to the cool water, and she didn't stop there, trailing her digit down, down, tracing the ridges of his abs until she reached the waist of his swimming trunks. "I really, really appreciate it.

He growled low in his throat. "Paige."

"What?" She blinked up at him, all innocence, but he caught the gleam in her eyes. "You don't want me to show you my appreciation?"

"If you show me any more appreciation, we're likely to be arrested," he croaked out, past the anticipation that tightened his throat.

"Nonsense," she replied cheerfully. "We're hidden here, and you wouldn't let anything bad happen to me, would you?"

"Never," he declared fiercely.

"Perfect." She smiled at him, and it was like the sun, reaching out and warming every inch of his skin, even in the tiny cave. She palmed him through his trunks and he closed his eyes to keep from coming too fast. Everything with Paige felt hotter, urgent, more intense. The flames licked at his skin, spreading up from his throbbing cock and sending warmth rushing through his chest. Then she was reaching up, tugging his head down to her, their lips meeting in a scorching kiss. Groaning deep in his throat, Mareko caught her up in his arms, revelling in the soft press of her body, his hands roaming down to squeeze the luscious curve of her backside. She gasped, winding her legs around his waist, pressing her core against his length and all the blood left in Mareko's body gave up trying to keep him functioning and tunnelled south instead.

"You feel amazing," Paige whispered as he trailed kisses down her sternum, nudging aside one of the triangles that had tormented him for days and fastening his mouth to the tip of one perfect breast.

*He* felt amazing? No, it was her. She was perfection. He'd found heaven here between her thighs, nirvana in the creamy cushion of her breasts. He was Mohammed, finding enlightenment in a cave, and he would serve no deity but Paige Beckett for the rest of his days.

She was... she was pushing his head away. Why was she pushing his head away?

"Stop, stop," she panted and it took every ounce of willpower he possessed to do so.

"Can you hear that?"

Above them, muffled by the water, a familiar refrain.

"Dad?"

Rosa had made it to the waterfall.

Quickly Mareko untangled himself from paradise. His body protested, but the only thing he was more reluctant to do than stop was to let his daughter catch him in a compromising position.

"Oh shit," Paige's eyes were wide. "What do we do?"

Mareko didn't answer, diving underwater instead and kicking out through the water to the pool beyond. He rolled over onto his back, taking care to keep the lower half of his body deep beneath the surface. At the top of the rock slide, Rosa peered down at him.

"I couldn't see you!"

"I was showing Paige the cave."

"There's a cave?" Rosa's eyes lit up. "Can I see?"

"Of course. Slide on down and I'll show you."

"Two seconds, I want to get some momentum." She disappeared from view, and Mareko transferred his attention to the bottom of the fall in time to see Paige bob up, her bikini firmly in place.

"She's okay?"

"She's fine. She wants to get her speed up."

Paige threw her head back, her laugh bouncing around the high stone walls. "Of course she does." She swam further out and turned to face the waterfall, cheering as Rosa came tumbling down in a tangle of limbs and laughter, catching her up in a hug as she surfaced. And for the first time since he'd moved back to Samoa, Mareko wondered if maybe what he'd always assumed was love was in fact lust. Because this? This was a whole lot different to anything he'd ever felt before.

# CHAPTER 10

Mareko hummed as he sat at his desk the next day, sunlight streaming in through the garden window. He'd opened it for once—air conditioning be damned—and the scent of frangipani floated in on the breeze, along with the vanilla undernotes of the pancakes being flipped fresh on the griddle of the breakfast fale.

Everything was falling into place. After the sliding rocks yesterday, where he'd snapped a few photos of Rosa to replace the younger ones of her in his office, and a couple of Paige backlit in gold, they'd returned to The Moananui and he'd received a phone call from the hospital. His father was on the mend and they were talking about sending him back to his care facility at the end of the week. Mareko knew Enele would have preferred to return to the resort, but his father was practical about the circumstances. His health conditions, especially now in the wake of a heart attack and surgery meant that Enele would likely not return to The Moananui for anything longer than day visits. Mareko had used the profits of the sale of Hélène's Paris apartment to set up a trust for Rosa, with a small amount securing a villa in the best retirement village nearby. When it was time, Penina would move in with Enele too, and they could live out the rest of their days in a safe environment, cared for by professionals while still maintaining their independence. It wasn't strictly fa'a Samoa—the Samoan way—but Enele and Penina Osa were nothing if not ruthlessly practical. It was their realistic approach to life that had led them to develop Mareko's grandfather's resort into world-class accommodation, and instilled the traits of sensibility and self-sacrifice in Mareko himself.

He didn't feel all that sensible at the moment though. He felt like a teenager again, almost giddy with anticipation to finish his work for the day and join his family. To visit his father with Rosa and his mum, then return home to sit around the dining table, talking and laughing as they chowed down on delicious food. They'd order from the restaurant tonight, he decided. No need for his mother or Paige to put themselves out.

Then, when Penina and Rosa retired for the evening, he could order drinks delivered to the bungalow. A coconut margarita for Paige, or perhaps a bottle of champagne. He'd done that again last night and the two of them had sat on the deck, sipping their drinks in the purple-tinted night, lit by the citronella candles and moonlight while they talked about anything and everything.

He'd told her about Hélène. How she'd left him before she passed. More than he'd told his parents even. She'd confided more of her cancer journey—the difficult details that painted her face in shadow as she spoke them aloud, but also about the way it had affected her growing up. The things she'd missed out on, both as a result of her treatment and as her parents' need to protect her shifted from concern to overwhelm. When their drinks were finished, he'd led her by the hand to his bedroom and kissed away the furrow between her blonde brows before proving to her exactly how resilient he thought she was with each snap of his hips and drag of his teeth against her satin skin.

He'd never been so grateful his family was full of deep sleepers.

"Hey." A soft voice interrupted his carnal thoughts, and he looked up to see the woman he was fantasising about hovering in the doorway.

"Good morning, lo'u alofa." He peered behind her into the hallway. "Where's Rosa?"

"She's got an important meeting with Iosefa," Paige replied, making her way into his office and sitting on one of the aqua chairs in front of his desk. "She scheduled it with him and everything." Her eyes crinkled at the corners as she smiled fondly. "She doesn't want me there, said it's something she has to do on her own."

Mareko huffed out a laugh. "That sounds about right. Do you know what this meeting is about?"

"I believe she's force-feeding him coconut-lime macarons and trying to convince him to hire her for kitchen prep duties twice a week making pie fillings and such."

"Ah, my pepe," Mareko shook his head, admiration coursing through him. "She'll run the world one day. This world at least."

Paige's smile widened. "She will. She's an incredible kid."

"Even more incredible now," Mareko replied sincerely. "I want to thank you for everything you've done for her since you arrived. I know nannying wasn't how you'd planned to spend your vacation, but Rosa has blossomed under your care. She's always been vivacious, but now..." his lips tugged upwards as he remembered her demonstrating infant CPR on a stuffed giraffe several nights ago, "she's a force. It's been a hard couple of years for her, but I see her resilience returning, her inner strength. A lot of that comes from you. She watches you, imitates you in many ways. I'm glad she has such a strong woman in her life as a role model."

Paige's cheeks pinked. "I don't think it has anything to do with me," she protested. "Rosa is stronger than I ever was. If anything, she inspires me. She makes me want to be better, to overcome my own insecurities."

Mareko shrugged. "Let's agree to disagree. Either way, she's loved having you here these holidays. *I've* loved having you here these holidays." He didn't miss the flicker of heat in her eyes and part of him thrilled. He'd spoken the L word aloud and she hadn't run screaming. Perhaps there was a chance she felt the same.

Nerves coiling in his stomach, he opened his mouth. "Paige, I–"

"Boss?" Rachel knocked on the door frame, poking her head into the office. "The travel blogger we're comping for their stay has pulled up. You told me to let you know when they arrived?"

"Fa'afetai, Rachel." Mareko stood, adjusting his tie. He'd reached out to a famous social-media blogger with a focus on sustainable tourism prior to Paige's wedding, hoping to capitalise on the publicity of the *One True Love* finale. The resort had offered to put them up for free if they'd be interested in coming to write about Samoa. Now that the finale hadn't taken place quite as expected, it was even more essential that the visit went well.

"I need to attend to this," he informed Paige as he stepped around his desk. "I'll see you at home later?"

"Sure thing."

Checking that Rachel had departed, he lowered his head and planted a lingering kiss on Paige's lips.

"I'll be back around three to take Rosa and Mum to the hospital," he murmured. "Until then, lo'u alofa."

The blush on her cheeks was enough to have him smiling all the way to the lobby.

"Mareko Osa?" A willowy brunette in a tank top and loose-fitting pants printed with constellations approached him, hand outstretched. "A pleasure to meet you."

"The pleasure is all mine. Madison Longley, I presume?"

Madison smiled toothily and whipped out a sheaf of documents. For all her bohemian style, chunky silver bracelets and the fine line tattoos parading up and down her arms, there was no doubt this was a shrewd businesswoman. Mareko led her to one of the white wicker sofas scattered across the lobby to discuss the details of her stay, more than impressed by the blogger's tenacity and attention to detail.

Twenty minutes later, Madison was checked into the bridal suite Paige had first stayed in when she arrived at The Moananui, and Mareko was back at his desk. His email pinged as soon as he woke his computer up and he navigated to his inbox to investigate. One thing that had been drummed into him in his hotel management courses was that an organised inbox meant an organised business, and while The Moananui might still be clawing its way back from the brink of financial ruin. Mareko had yet to see evidence to the contrary. The Lord himself knew what state the resort would be in if he wasn't on top of correspondence.

Seeing his lawyer's name in the subject line, Mareko's brow furrowed. He clicked on the email and skimmed over it, only to stop in shock and anger, returning to the greeting to read through carefully from the top once more.

"You've got to be shitting me." His own disbelief reverbed through the office, cold and hollow. He read the email once more, just to make sure he hadn't missed anything. Hell, just to make sure he wasn't imagining it. He wasn't. It was laid out there on his screen in black and white.

The production company for *One True Love* was suing him.

"AND THEN IOSEFA said that I can make the supo esi for the Sunday breakfast buffet!" Rosa's excitement echoed off the bungalow walls.

"That's wonderful news!" Paige pulled the girl in for a hug. "I'm so proud of you!"

"He's going to supervise me," Rosa added, her nose wrinkling in distaste. "But I suppose it's better than nothing."

Paige smothered her laugh. "It's a great compromise," she declared. "I know it's a simple dish, but it's for a lot of people and you are only nine, Rosa."

"Ten next month!" Rosa gestured to the year-long calendar pinned on the kitchen bulletin board. One square was firmly decorated with glittery borders and the number ten in bright pink digits.

"Ten is still a very impressive age to be let loose in a commercial kitchen," Paige assured her. "I'm twenty-seven and I still haven't achieved that."

"Ooh, we should make something in there before you go! Then you'll have done it!" Rosa rattled on about when they might be able to get time in the big resort kitchen, but Paige's mind was stuck on her words.

*Before you go.*

That was the thing, wasn't it? She was leaving. Despite the sense of belonging she'd found at The Moananui, she still had to head back to her real life in New Zealand. It would be madness not to—even a child like Rosa accepted it as fact. Paige had a job, a flat, a *life* waiting for her in another country at the bottom of the Pacific.

Her heart twisted.

*It's for the best*, she reminded herself. No matter how much she might want to stay, the truth was that The Moananui was merely a stop on her journey. An unplanned stop, even. She could never have predicted when she packed her bag for Samoa three weeks ago, when she'd laid her bead-encrusted wedding gown carefully across the top of her suitcase safely swaddled in its garment bag, that she'd still be here. Unmarried, with her reminders of Patrick nothing but a fading tan line on her ring finger and a bad taste in her mouth.

Yet she *was* here. And somehow this experience, which had been intended to be an escape from the media scrutiny and her own mistakes, had given her the greatest joy she'd felt in her life.

She was in love, she realised, heart thudding in her chest. With Samoa. With Rosa.

With Mareko.

With the life she'd built here, even without meaning to.

Bliss flooded her body and she reached across to pull a still-chattering Rosa into a hug.

"What's happening?" Rosa squeaked, her face squished against Paige's upper arm.

"I love you," Paige declared, dropping a kiss on Rosa's hair, inhaling the scent of the coconut oil Penina combed through it each evening.

"I love you, too." Rosa pecked her on the cheek and

Paige almost floated away in her happiness. "Now, what do you think about learning how to make chop suey?"

"Whatever you want," Paige smiled. Her heart was full to bursting, but underneath it all ran an undercurrent of tension. Mareko had been hurt so deeply in the past—would he even be open to love again? And with her? Someone who had stumbled so dramatically into his life, clad in wedding corsetry escaping a groom she'd publicly abandoned. Everything she knew about Mareko spoke to his perfectionism and after years of cataloguing her flaws, Paige was deeply aware of how far from perfect she was.

*All you can do is tell him*, she affirmed silently. *You can't control how he'll feel, but you can choose to be brave enough to share your feelings with him.*

As she thought it, the bungalow door flew open. Mareko stood outlined in the doorway, his face tight with anger.

"Papa? What's wrong?"

Mareko's eyes skimmed past Rosa to land on Paige. "I'm being sued."

"What?" Paige stumbled to her feet. "Who's suing you?"

"Trinity Productions." His voice rang with bitterness and her heart sank as realisation took hold.

"Because of the wedding."

"No, Paige. Not because of the wedding. Because of the fact that there was *no* wedding."

Paige sank back onto the sofa, one hand pressed to her chest as if to ease the deafening thump of her heart.

"I don't understand. The resort..."

Mareko gave a tight shake of his head. "The resort has insurance. It will likely be negotiated away. They'll refuse to pay of course, despite the extra staff we hired for the weekend, all the food we ordered in. All we'll be left with is the deposit, although I'll be surprised if they don't try and claim that back as well. But they've named me personally in the suit. Apparently someone saw you leaving the lobby with me before the wedding was due to start, and I'm being personally held liable for my role in preventing the event taking place, breaching the conditions of the contract I signed with the production company."

Paige's chest wrenched tighter as he spoke.

"You had no idea," she protested, but Mareko held up a hand to silence her, the line of his jaw tight with fury.

"It doesn't matter what I knew. I signed a contract stating the wedding could take place here, and then I hid the bride before the ceremony." His eyes darted back to Rosa. "Rosa, can you please run up to the spa and ask your tinamatua to come straight back after her massage? I need to talk about this with her and your tamamatua."

Rosa nodded, round eyes solemn in her small face. Mareko waited until she'd left before speaking again, though Paige could feel the tension rolling off him in waves.

"For God's sake," he hissed, running a hand through his hair as the door banged shut behind Rosa, "I'm fucking you!"

Paige's blood turned to ice. "I wasn't engaged when we started sleeping together."

"That doesn't matter! Think of the optics. I squirrelled a bride who was due to be married at my resort away minutes before her ceremony and seduced her. No matter what happened between you and Patrick, I couldn't have done anything stupider. Who will book their weddings here now?" His dark eyes flashed wild in his face and dragged an open palm across his jaw.

"Mareko." She moved towards him, grasping his hands in hers to keep them from tunnelling through his hair, and squeezing, willing him to calm down through her touch.

There was a solution, of course there was. They just had to find it. "We can fix this."

He laughed, but there was no humour in it.

"How do you propose we fix it, Paige? Even if this doesn't ruin the resort financially – and that's a big if – our reputation will be tarnished. If the slightest hint of this gets out The Moananui will be the laughingstock of the Pacific."

"I can help. I can talk to the producers–" she stopped suddenly as the idea struck her. *Natalia.* "I can fix this," Paige continued firmly. "Mareko, look at me."

He met her eyes, and she saw the moment he believed her. His mouth softened and his breathing slowed, that broad chest relaxing as he exhaled deeply.

"I can fix this," she repeated, and he nodded.

"Okay."

"I need to make some calls. Why don't you go find your mother and take her for a cup of tea in the pavilion? Who knows what Rosa's told her? She might need a bit of calming down. I'll come and find you when I've finished."

Mareko nodded slowly.

"Trust me," Paige urged, reaching up to cup his jaw. "Please."

"I do. I do trust you, Paige." He covered her hand with his own, and turned his face to press a kiss to his palm. "I'll see you in the pavilion."

"I won't even be an hour," she assured him. "Have some 'ava. You look like you need it."

Mareko closed his eyes but a smile tugged at the corners of his lips and hope soared in Paige. She could do this, she could take away his worries with a simple phone call. Mareko would relax and his family could be assured their legacy wasn't in jeopardy.

Paige wasn't stupid and neither was Natalia. The

producer didn't want money, she wanted a story. All Paige had to do was negotiate on the behalf of The Moananui Resort a little.

Natalia picked up on the first ring.

"Hello?"

"Natalia. It's Paige Beckett."

There was a pause, then a low whistle. "Well, well. Look who's finally back online." A thread of smugness wound its way through her tone, like a line of cream through black ink.

Paige took a deep breath. "Yes. About that."

It took forty minutes of cajoling, and letting Natalia berate her before they reached an agreement. Paige would catch a flight back next week and show up 'unannounced' at Patrick's door to apologise for her inexcusable behaviour – all on camera of course. They'd do the reunion episode that was already scheduled, and Paige would offer her blessing and support for Patrick to move on with the runner-up, Jacqui. Privately, Paige thought Jacqui was too good for Patrick, but the other girl had seemed genuinely distressed at the wrap party after Patrick and Paige had announced their engagement. Hopefully, Patrick would find her interesting enough that he wouldn't need to fake his feelings for her.

After Natalia grudgingly agreed to send through the details of the new plan and call off her lawyers, Paige hung up and headed towards the main resort. Success and love made her buoyant, and she bounced along the well-trod dirt path, riding the high of having avoided causing Mareko and his family distress. Her behaviour had resulted in a problem, yes, but she'd fixed it. More importantly, Mareko had trusted her to fix it. Trusted that she had the skills and smarts to do what was needed. Paige hugged herself as she strode through the lobby. If he trusted her, then chances were he could grow to love her. She would tell him how she felt tonight and let the chips fall where they may.

*Snap.*

A photographer jumped out from behind a potted palm. "Paige! Look here!" She was blinded by the flash of a camera, then another and another. Blinking her eyes against the onslaught, she cleared her vision in time to see a small white man in scruffy shorts and a garish floral print shirt approach her, his phone outstretched.

"Why'd you leave Patrick at the altar? Was he on drugs? Did he cheat on you? Did you cheat on him?"

"What?' Paige's brain scrambled to keep up, to process this sudden turn of events. After three weeks of press silence, she wasn't even remotely prepared for this. She was in her bathing suit, for Pete's sake! "No. How did you find me?"

The journalist cackled. "It wasn't hard. You're on the resort's social media feed, love." He moved closer and she could see his phone was recording. This was going to be all over the Internet in minutes.

*Shit.* Her temporary anonymity was gone, smashed into smithereens by…

"Did you say the resort posted pictures of me?"

"Sure did." He snapped his gum in her face. "What message do you want to send old Paddy boy, huh? Are we going for careless floozy on a tropical holiday? Heartbroken hermit communing with nature?" He raked his eyes up and down Paige's body and her skin crawled. "Ice queen who stomped all over his heart? Give me an exclusive and I'll paint whatever picture you want."

Paige's heart stalled. "No, thank you," she managed, skirting around the unwelcome intruder. "Rachel?"

"On it," the concierge was already moving towards the reporter, signalling one of the strapping young men behind the counter as she went.

Paige escaped the lobby, the warm rush of tropical air doing nothing to soothe the chill in her bones as she rushed towards the bungalow. Bursting through the door, she snatched up her phone from beside her bed and typed in 'The Moananui Resort', navigating to the social media links.

There she was, alright.

Exhaling shakily, Paige plopped down on her bed, goosebumps racing across her skin. A long shot of her in her yellow bikini, in all her pear-shaped glory. She'd never exposed her thighs publicly before - even on *One True Love* she'd remained covered up on the bottom half - long skirts and dresses, or sarongs if she was in swimwear. Now everything was out there on the Internet for anyone to see. For anyone to comment on. Her face was thrown back and she was smiling, the rare, genuine smile she hadn't used for a photo since she was fourteen, when the illusion of her happiness became more important than the reality. She was so focused on that, on the way she looked, it took a minute for her to notice the photo's background.

She was standing on craggy grey-brown rock, lush green bush creeping down from the top of the photograph to form nature's very own backdrop. Crystal clear water covered her feet, a hint of white-tipped excitement to the left of her.

*The sliding rocks.*

There was only one person who could have taken this picture, one person there with her that day who had a phone.

One person who had readily admitted that he would do anything to restore the reputation of his resort, to protect his daughter's future.

Nausea slammed against Paige's ribs. *Not again.*

She couldn't have been fooled again, could she? Not by Mareko.

Her heart railed against the idea, but her brain insisted, flashing through every instance she'd quashed her own feelings to protect someone else's, every time she'd been naive enough to believe the best in others while they used and discarded her. For study notes, fame, now fortune apparently.

*No*, she told herself firmly. *The definition of madness is doing the same thing over and over again and expecting different results.*

Paige Bennett had been burned before, but fire raged in her soul now, hot and angry, searing the backs of her eyelids as she blinked away tears. She was sick of being a pawn in people's lives. The facts remained. Mareko had taken that photograph, he was in charge of social media for the resort, and it was there on their feed. There was only one rational conclusion, and only one logical course of action.

She was done.

# CHAPTER 11

"Gone?" Mareko's voice filled the lobby of The Moananui. Guests stopped and stared but he was too incensed to care. "What do you mean she's gone?"

"Exactly what I said." Rachel was inputting data into the computer, ignoring his histrionics with the practised boredom of someone used to withstanding tantrums on a regular basis. "She left. Called a taxi to take her to the airport."

"Why didn't you call me?"

"And say what, Mareko?" Rachel eyed him steadily. "That a grown adult was leaving the property? Is that the kind of information you expect about the women in your life?"

Mareko growled. The girl code was strong with this one, but he was in no mood to appreciate the show of solidarity.

"She left a note," Rachel offered casually, as if this wasn't momentous news. She held up a slip of paper and he grabbed at it eagerly. He opened it, butterflies swarming in his stomach as he recognised Paige's neat handwriting on the hotel stationery.

*To Mareko, Rosa and Penina,*

*Thank you so much for your hospitality during my time in Samoa. I could not have imagined a better family to spend my time with. I'm afraid a situation has arisen which requires my immediate return to New Zealand. I apologise for not being able to say goodbye in person.*

*Paige*

*PS: Mareko, the legal situation has been resolved. I hope my time here has been as useful for you as you had hoped.*

Mareko's head buzzed. That was it? Three weeks of joy and laughter, three weeks of bringing light into his life, of bringing *love* into his life, and that was it? And she hoped she had been *useful*?

The familiar gnaw in his gut began, roiling to a boil the way it had when he'd realised Hélène didn't love him.

*It's happening again.*

His insides had been scooped out, leaving him hollow, a faint ringing in his ears. He'd done it again, taken a risk on another woman who didn't love him, only to be left behind with nothing ahead of him but bleak nights comforting his daughter as she sobbed into a pillow.

*No.* No, Paige would never do that. It was unthinkable. Unacceptable. There was a reason for her departure, and he would find it. If she didn't love him, he could cope with that. He'd been there before. But he loved her. He would fight for her. And if her answer was still no, she would need to tell him to his face. He was no Patrick, no simpering smarmy sycophant desperate for adulation from adoring fans, ready to throw his relationship away based on the scratching of some ink on paper. He was a man – *her* man – and she could damn well tell him if she didn't want him. At least he'd have tried. If there was one thing he'd learned in the dreadful destruction of his marriage, it was that he didn't want regrets hanging over him every day, and letting Paige Beckett go without a reason would be the greatest regret of his life.

"Can you please call me a car?" He gritted the question out. "I need to leave immediately."

Rachel pasted her customer service smile on. "Of course, sir. I'll have one here in fifteen minutes."

He hurried to the bungalow, grabbing an overnight bag from the top of his wardrobe and shoving a couple of pairs of socks, underwear and t-shirts inside, along with his toothbrush, body wash, passport and wallet.

He was reaching for his phone charger when his phone buzzed with a message from Rachel.

*Car's here.*

Throwing the charger in his bag and zipping it, he started back towards the lobby, more determined than ever to seek answers.

But when he stepped from the cool gleaming lobby to the fading afternoon light, he was the one peppered with questions.

"Mr Osa? How long has Paige Beckett been staying at The Moananui Resort? Are you responsible for her decision to leave Patrick Winslow at the altar? What do you think about the rumours that he's trying to win her back? Is she working as an official spokesperson for the resort?"

Mareko reared back, raising a hand to block the reporter's camera.

"Rachel," he bellowed over his shoulder.

"*Ioe.* I'm on it." She was there in an instant with Loto, one of the desk clerks who worked out like a demon in addition to being the lead performer in fiafia nights. Loto had no trouble muscling the paunchy white man down the circular driveway towards the main road.

He climbed into the waiting car, and gave his destination, pulling his phone out to check the international flight schedule. He'd had it on silent today, wanting to make the most of his time with Rosa. Even so, he was surprised by the ream of notifications clogging his home screen. Opening the most prominent social media site, he saw why.

Why his phone was blowing up.

Why there was a reporter at The Moananui.

Why Paige had left him.

She looked beautiful, head thrown back in laughter, the light playing across her features like God himself was smiling down on her. Her yellow bikini popped against the lush green foliage behind her, water bubbling at her feet. It was a stunning candid shot. And it was posted by The Moananui.

Paige Beckett, minor celebrity in hiding, was front and centre, the caption in both English and Samoan promoting the sliding rocks and resort in the same sentence, drawing a clear line between the woman and her chosen refuge.

Mareko's stomach dropped. The final sentence of Paige's note made sense now. She thought he'd posted it. She thought he'd used her – her image at least – without her consent, to promote his business interests.

It wasn't that the thought hadn't crossed his mind in the early days of their acquaintance. But now? He would never. He'd seen her devastation in the wake of Patrick betraying her privacy in the media. She had to know he would never do that to her.

His own words, spoken before he'd admitted his own feelings to himself, came back to haunt him.

*"My family and this resort's success are the only things that matter."*

No wonder she had run, thinking he was yet another person who had put his own goals ahead of her.

He had to get to her. He had to explain. They could work through this.

He made it to the airport with minutes to spare in catching the final flight of the day, handing over his credit card to snag one of the last unoccupied seats – business class, because that was his poor luck today – without so much as a wince. The flight to Auckland was packed, but no sooner had he taken his seat the captain announced delays in takeoff to a cacophony of resounding groans through the cabin.

Mareko didn't mind. He stared unseeingly at the movie playing on another passenger's screen, tapping his fingers against his knee until the eventual takeoff, then dozed for a couple of hours. When he awoke, he used the plane's WiFi to connect to his emails, noting the one from Trinity Productions informing him that they were no longer pursuing legal recourse.

*She did it.*

Relief swelled over him. Paige had said she would take care of the lawsuit – she'd said she had, actually, in that poor excuse for a goodbye note – and he'd trusted her, but seeing it on his screen in black and white was something else. Part of his tension melted away. Paige wouldn't have done that for someone she didn't care about. Hope flared to life in him again.

It was that hope that sustained him all the way through the remainder of the flight, through the disembarkment in the indigo light of early morning and through passport control. It was that hope that led him out into Arrivals, his carryon slung over his shoulder as he thumbed through his phone, trying to divine the next steps to get him to Paige's hometown of Rotorua. He'd shamelessly asked Rachel to mine the guest files for Paige's address from the plane, and had no regrets about it.

It was that hope that died a swift and brutal death moments later when a commotion ahead caught his attention and he looked up to see the woman of his dreams standing in front of her scumbag ex, who was bent on one knee, the diamond ring in his hand glinting under the artificial lights while camera operators surrounded them and a small woman with dark hair gave them an enthusiastic thumbs up.

*Wait!* The voice inside him screamed. It sounded like his father's voice, but it could easily have been that of past misdeeds trying to torture him. *Just wait!*

So Mareko waited. He waited and watched while Patrick stood, a slimy smirk creeping over his face. Then he watched as the other man reached over and pulled Paige into an embrace right there in the Arrivals hall, as people stopped to take photographs of the pair. His heart dropped into his shoes and he turned away.

He couldn't watch anymore.

She was gone. And so was any hope of her loving him in return.

# CHAPTER 12

The smell hit Paige the instant she stepped off the plane.

*Home.*

No place on Earth smelt like Aotearoa New Zealand. It wasn't something she noticed in her day-to-day life, but the moment she stepped foot back on the soil – tarmac, really – of her home country, it flooded her senses and she breathed in greedily. Paige hadn't travelled overseas much in her life. Samoa, of course. A couple of trips to Australia in high school and university, and a fortnight in Cambodia after she'd finished her doctorate as a treat before the tortuous two years she'd spent as a house officer before gaining her general practitioner qualification.

But every time she returned, that unique scent hit her olfactory sense like a shot of dopamine to her soul.

And boy, did she need a hit of dopamine. The three-hour flight to Auckland she'd managed to secure a cheap economy seat on upon arriving at Faleolo International Airport had been delayed for hours. From here, she still had a short flight back to Rotorua, then a forty-minute drive to her small town.

Wearily, she followed her fellow passengers as they made their way through passport control to the baggage claim, then through customs. A few people pointed at her, whispering to their companions and the Māori woman who sold her an enormous bottle of vodka in duty free grinned at her.

"Bet you need this after the last few weeks, love."

"You have no idea," Paige assured her fervently, slipping a box of chocolates onto the counter beside it. Two breakups in less than a month. She was going to wallow properly, dammit. She still had a week before she was scheduled to return to work. Lily had never liked Patrick, surely her flatmate would be keen to toast his departure from their lives.

Then she was out in Arrivals, dragging her suitcase across the polished tile as she headed towards the exit and the domestic terminal.

"Paige! Paige!"

The sound of her name echoed through the arrivals hall in the early morning hush. Spinning on her heel, Paige searched the thinning crowd for the source.

*Oh, for fuck's sake...*

"Patrick?"

He was running towards her, but slowly. She squinted, trying to make sense of his odd movements, before catching a glimpse of the camera operators training their lenses on him. *One True Love* camera operators, if her eyes didn't deceive her.

Of course. Far be it from her to be able to return to her home country on a dawn flight without being accosted by her fame-hungry ex-fiancé, and... was that Natalia behind him?

Paige crossed her arms and waited. Of all the trite, pointless exercises...

Patrick arrived in front of her moments later, and swept her up in his arms.

Startled, Paige pushed at his shoulder. "Let me down, you great oaf!"

He did, but immediately dropped to a knee in front of her, clasping both of her hands in his.

"Paige," he began, and apprehension roiled through her.

"What are you doing?" she hissed, but he ignored her, projecting his voice so that people in the near vicinity stopped to listen.

"I made a mistake, darling. I'm begging you to forgive me. Can you give us another chance?" Releasing one of her hands, he dug in his pants pocket, pulling out the clunky, halo-set diamond ring he'd first proposed with. "Please, Paige. Say you'll take me back."

"Are you serious?" Paige crouched down so she could speak without being overheard. "Patrick, what on earth is going on?"

"Optics," he whispered back. "There's a presenter role coming up and I need the public's support. Natalia told me about the new plan, but then she got a call from a reporter in Samoa saying he saw you boarding this flight. We figured, why not double down on my rejection to get people onside."

Paige clenched her teeth. "By proposing *again*? You didn't even want to marry me the first time!"

"You don't know that!" Patrick protested.

"I do so! I heard you telling Natalia before our wedding."

Patrick's expression cleared. "So that's why you ran away. I wondered. It didn't seem like you."

Paige rolled her eyes. "Can you please stand up? People are looking."

Patrick got to his feet, brushing his pants off and pocketing the ring. "Did you get that?" he called over to Natalia, who gave him a thumbs up.

"Great." He turned back to look at Paige. "You look well. Did you have a nice time on our honeymoon?"

"Yes, it was lovely," Paige replied tartly. "Better for not having to spend it with a man who had no interest in me." Her heart clenched at the lie but she lifted her chin and glared at Patrick, who cocked an eyebrow in response.

"Well, look who got a spine along with her suntan. What did you think was going to happen, Paige? You honestly thought I would fall in love with someone in six weeks? That's not realistic."

*I fell in love with Mareko in three*, Paige thought uncharitably, but the thought hurt so much she pushed it aside.

"Why weren't you honest with me?" she asked instead.

Patrick shrugged. "Why weren't you?" he countered. "You didn't really want me. You wanted *someone*. It felt like who that someone was didn't matter much as long as they were ready to settle down and help you pop out some kids."

Paige stilled, his words reaching inside her and flicking a switch. Realisation dawned.

"You're right," she finally managed. "I'm sorry. If I'd been honest with myself from the start, then perhaps I would have been able to be more honest with you. And I apologise for leaving you at the altar. I was angry and hurt, but that's no excuse. I should have talked to you properly about it."

Patrick shrugged again. He looked like a marionette. "Doesn't matter. This jilted groom persona has been serving me alright. I've got a few things lined up that Natalia is going to help me capitalise on."

"That's good, I guess?" Paige couldn't imagine a world in which heartbreak, even perceived heartbreak, was the cornerstone to a successful career, but since falling in love with Mareko her bitterness towards Patrick had melted away.

"I wish you the best, then," she said, and he smiled, the genuine smile she'd seen him wear on his dates with the runner-up Jacqui.

"Thanks, Paige. You too." Patrick pulled her in for a hug and she let him, grinding her teeth when he patted her on the head like a biddable labrador as they separated.

Paige headed out into the crisp early morning air, rolling her bag along behind her as she made her way over towards the domestic terminal. Dewdrops glistened on the fronds of the native flax planted sporadically along the path, the leaves of a few taller trees painted in shades of green. A tide of longing for Samoa washed over Paige as she walked, making her way through exhaust fumes and around the airport parking garage. She missed the islands.

No, she corrected herself, not the islands. She missed Mareko. The wave of fury that had swept her out of Samoa had ebbed, leaving behind an insistent ache in her heart. The chill in her bones had nothing to do with the temperature, and everything to do with the man she'd left behind.

*He let you leave,* her traitorous mind whispered, but that thought hurt even more. Once again, her thoughts, her needs, had been overlooked by someone who professed to care for her. Her vision blurred, and she swiped the tears away, but her memories would not be dismissed so easily.

She remembered the care he'd shown towards her, the way he'd given her that full, gorgeous laugh, how he'd come to her seeking comfort after Enele's heart attack, the gentle way he'd laid her down at night and made her beg until he covered her body with his and she lost herself in him.

She was lost now, alright. Her feet might be on familiar soil, but her heart? That was back at The Moananui.

Once in the domestic terminal, she checked her bag and ordered an oat latte. She'd cut caffeine from her diet in the lead up to the wedding and hadn't bothered reintroducing it while she was working at The Moananui—not with their delicious selection of teas, smoothies and fresh pressed juices. But she was back in the real world now—her real world. Back to Rotorua, and practising medicine and watching general knowledge quiz shows with Lily on the sagging floral couch in their flat. Suddenly, she needed a coffee very badly.

It tasted terrible.

Sighing, she chucked it in the bin, careful to check that the barista who'd handed it to her wasn't watching. No to coffee, then. Some things might have changed more than she'd realised.

She got another reminder of that two hours later when she unlocked the door to her and Lily's flat, to find Lily bent over the floral couch in front of a strapping man wearing half a rugby kit, getting absolutely railed.

"Fuck me! I mean, no... don't... shit, sorry! I'm going!" Paige retreated quickly, slamming the door shut behind her and wrestling her panicked laughter into submission until she was firmly ensconced behind the wheel of her car.

Limited in her options, she pulled out onto the highway and pointed her car south towards her parent's farm. She really needed to let them know she was home, and apologise in person for the wedding fiasco. She couldn't regret her actions though. Mareko might have broken her heart, but he'd given her so much too. Confidence. Clarity. The kind of passion that sustained her through the days and lit up her nights. Pain lanced her as she drove. She couldn't reconcile the image of the man who had shown her such pleasure with the stone-faced businessman who'd told her she was nothing more than an employee. Had she imagined it all? Had her desire to be loved, to be *wanted*, for more than her name, her brain, her body fooled her into believing he felt more for her than he did?

Thirty minutes later she pulled up the gravel drive of her parent's farmhouse, barely missing the elderly Jack Russell who lumbered out of the way in a habit born of experience and self-preservation.

"Hey, Walter," she called as she exited the car, bending down to scritch under his grey-flecked ears.

"Paige? Honey, is that you?" Her mother's voice floated down the porch steps and wrapped itself around Paige in a too-tight hug. The boa constrictor of greetings, cutting off her air supply as her imagination provided a slideshow of all the ways she'd disappointed her parents since she walked out on Patrick in Samoa.

"There you are!" Kathleen Beckett rounded the back of Paige's car. "What are you doing down there? Stand up and come inside." Kathleen wrapped her arms around Paige as she stood, and Paige breathed in the scent of lavender and baby powder. She'd brought her mother designer perfume for Mother's Day last year and Kathleen had ooh'ed over it, but as far as Paige was aware it was still in the bathroom cabinet, the stopper sealed.

"Hi Mum," Paige leaned into the hug a moment, seeking

comfort, but Kathleen whirled away and headed for the house.

"I'll call your father," she said over her shoulder. "He'd like to see you."

Sure enough, the women had barely sat down at the wooden dining table with their steaming cups of tea and a plate of shortbread when the front door eased open to reveal Gregory Beckett toeing off his work boots on the porch outside.

"Alright then, Paige?" He took a seat at the head of the table, and Kathleen slid his mug of tea over. He acknowledged her forethought with a nod of his head.

Paige had seen the same routine play out year after year, and out of the blue she was hit with a wave of desire for the kind of love her parents had. Perhaps their brand of love had bound her too tight, but there was no mistaking it, or their dedication to each other. Through every challenge - droughts, floods, infertility, a child with cancer, Kathleen and Gregory had remained steadfastly loyal, facing each new trial as a quiet team.

That's what Paige had been looking for on *One True Love*. What she had hoped to find. That was the kind of relationship she'd thought for a moment she might even have with Mareko – both of them flailing in their own way, but stronger united.

*Too bad you were wrong,* her internal voice taunted her. *He was using you, and you were so desperate to be loved for yourself you didn't even notice until a photographer jumped out of a potted palm.*

Paige took a hasty sip of tea, wincing as she burnt her tongue on the steaming beverage.

"How was Samoa?" Kathleen's voice was too bright, her

smile a little too wide, betraying the anxiety behind her cheery facade.

Paige lowered her mug. "You saw the news reports."

"Of course," Gregory answered gruffly. "That wanker Patrick was all over the news last night talking about making amends now you'd surfaced." He levelled a hard look at his daughter. "You're not going back to him, are you?"

"No," Paige sighed. She reached for the biscuit plate. If anything was going to ease the sting of this conversation, it was simple carbohydrates.

She took a bite. *Yum. Simple, alright. Simply delicious.*

"Good," Gregory grunted. "Didn't care much for him."

"I thought you liked Patrick." Paige couldn't hide her surprise. "I thought it was me you were upset with, for going on the show."

Gregory snorted. "No worries about that. But your taste in men left a bit to be desired."

"We wanted you to be happy," Kathleen interjected hurriedly before Paige could question her father further. "If Patrick made you happy, that was enough for us."

Gregory opened his mouth and Paige heard the distinct sound of someone being kicked under the table. He closed it again.

"But the show..." Paige said.

"Oh, that show was horrible!" Kathleen shuddered. "They made you look like such a simpleton. You're a doctor, for goodness' sake, and they edited it to make you look like a twit with a drinking habit. Shame on them," she continued, shaking her head. "That's not right. But you had agreed to marry Patrick by the time it finished airing, and you seemed happy enough." She shrugged. "That's all we wanted for you."

Tears pricked behind Paige's eyes. "I thought you were embarrassed by me."

"Embarrassed? Oh honey, no." Kathleen reached over and squeezed Paige's hand. "We were worried about you. You're not one to be impulsive, and the first we heard of this show was when you showed up on our porch with a camera crew. We didn't want to see you get hurt, is all. You've been through enough."

Paige turned the information over in her head, trying to see her interactions with her parents in the last few months through this new lens. It took very little effort to rework the narrative to fit with her mother's version of events. And if she'd been misreading those circumstances, what else might she have misconstrued?

"I can be impulsive, though," she said slowly, taking deep breaths to try and control her racing heart. "I work really hard not to be, to try not to cause you any extra stress. I've caused you enough worry over the years."

"What do you mean?" Kathleen's brow furrowed.

"I mean, I worry all the time about disappointing you. About not being enough. That's why I went into medicine after you wouldn't stop talking about the brilliant doctors who treated my cancer. It's why I never went to parties at uni, or protests, even for important things. Because what if something went wrong and I was hurt or arrested? I got all excited about theatre one year in high school and tried out for *The Sound of Music*. I was cast as Louisa. But then I started thinking about how much time it would take away from my academics, and what if I forgot my lines on stage and everyone laughed? You'd be so embarrassed."

Paige's parents blinked at her.

A sob rose in her throat. "It's even part of why I went on the show—to reassure you that I'd be okay if something ever happened to you. That I'd have someone who loved me, a child who loved me hopefully. That I'd be alright."

"Oh, Paige," Kathleen breathed. "How long have you felt this way?"

"As long as I can remember." The tears were flowing freely now, scalding her cheeks in thin streaks as they ran down to drip off her chin. "Definitely since the cancer."

Her mother said nothing, just squeezed her hand, tears pooling in her own eyes. Their mugs of tea sat to the side, forgotten.

"Poppycock!"

Startled, Paige turned to her father. "Dad?"

"This is absolute poppycock." Gregory turned watery blue eyes on her. "We love you, Paigey. I don't care if you're a doctor, or a florist, or working in a supermarket. Neither does your mother. I don't care if you're arrested for protesting or getting tipsy at parties, as long as you're safe. What does bother me is you feeling like you need to prove yourself to us." His voice gentled. "Paige, we've loved you since before you were born. Nothing is going to change that. The only thing – the *only* thing – that matters to us is your happiness. And right now, it sounds like you've been sacrificing that for years to give us what you thought we wanted." He reached out and tucked a strand of hair behind Paige's ear, the familiar callouses of his fingers brushing away a few errant tears. "We've got a lot to talk about, the three of us. It won't be easy, and it won't be fast, but nothing worth doing ever is. And this –" he gestured between the three of them " – is worth fixing."

"I don't know how to start," Paige admitted.

"None of us do, Paigey. So we'll do what we do every time there's a problem. We'll talk to the professionals. And they'll give us some tools to help us make a start. Can you do that for me?"

Paige nodded. She'd never have expected her rough, farmer father to suggest therapy, but now that he had, relief washed over her, sweeping away layers of fear and frustration that littered her soul like sediment.

"Yeah," she managed. "I can do that."

"Good," Gregory nodded. "Good. We'll look into that tomorrow. Now drink your tea and tell us what happened with that shitshow of a wedding."

# CHAPTER 13

*ne month later*

MAREKO LEANED on his elbows and rubbed the heels of his hands into his closed eyes. His deep sigh filled his office.

"Everything okay there, boss?"

"Everything's fine, thank you Rachel," he responded without looking.

Everything was not fine. Everything was a fucking mess. He was days behind on work. Paige's sudden departure a month ago had meant late starts and early finishes as his parenting duties took precedence. He loved spending time with Rosa, but the constant backlog of work piling up weighed on him. Enele had been moved back to his retirement village several days ago and Penina had spent hours each day since sitting by his bedside catching up on the gossip that had taken place in his absence while Mareko checked emails on his phone. Reporters had roamed the resort for weeks, refusing to move on even after Mareko had personally assured them Paige Beckett was no longer staying on the property. Beyond the logistics, the ache in his heart hadn't yet subsided. Everywhere he looked, he saw Paige. Saw her leaning against his desk, smiling at him. Saw her perched at the poolside bar, e-reader in hand.

He'd returned to Samoa in a fog, but once that cleared he'd realised he should have fought harder for her. He'd frozen in the moment, the way he had when Hélène left him, but he'd gritted his teeth against his newsfeeds filled with images of her and Patrick embracing at the airport to email her.

No response.

He should have known. When Paige decided on a course of action, she was unshakable. He respected that about her, but it didn't change the pain that knifed through him every time a memory of her heart-shaped face flashed through his mind.

A bowl of oka plonked down on his desk, interrupting his thoughts.

"What is this?" He looked up at Rachel, who was giving him the kind of disappointed look exclusive to mothers the world over.

"Lunch. Eat."

Mareko checked his watch. "It's three in the afternoon."

"And you missed lunch. So eat it. You have to leave in a few minutes to take Penina to visit your dad anyway and you'll likely be back here after that which means there's a chance you'll forget to eat dinner too."

It was true. There was no way he was getting to sleep before midnight tonight, not with the sudden uptick in occupancy. It galled him to admit it, but bookings had been up since The Moananui had been revealed as Paige's secret hideaway. Combined with the positive attention they'd received from Madison the travel blogger, The Moananui finally looked on track to reach its financial goals for the year for the first time since Mareko had discovered Edwin's betrayal.

He should be elated. But all he felt was empty and exhausted.

He forked up a chunk of fish and shoved it in his mouth, careful not to let coconut cream drip onto the restaurant sales report that sat in front of him.

"You can't carry on like this, Mareko," Rachel said softly, and he closed his eyes so he didn't have to look at her while he chewed.

"I know," he replied softly after he'd swallowed. "I know."

His concierge's warning hung over him as he collected his mother and Rosa from the bungalow twenty minutes later and drove them towards Enele's retirement village.

"Lo'u aiga!" The joy in his father's voice as they walked in brought a weak smile to Mareko's lips. Enele's spirits had been restored by returning to his assisted living facility, charming the nurses and rejoining other residents for tiak in the evenings.

He leaned against the wall by the door as Rosa chattered away to her grandfather, filling him in on the new school year, her teachers and her plans to join the girls' kilikiti team. Penina looked on indulgently, as she crocheted a blanket.

"Atali'i?"

Mareko's head shot up at the sound of his father summoning him.

"Tama?"

Enele eyed him steadily, and wariness crept over Mareko's skin.

"I need a moment alone with my son," he announced, and Rosa and Penina gathered up their things and filed out, shooting him sidelong glances as they went.

"What's wrong?"

Enele motioned at the armchair that sat next to his own. "Sit."

Mareko sat.

"You think I do not know my own son, hmmm? You think I do not see when you are unhappy?"

Mareko frowned down at his hands, folded in his lap. "I'm not unhappy."

"Pah! You come in here with a black cloud over you. What is so wrong in your life that spending time with your family puts that look on your face?"

"It's not you, Tama. I have a lot on my mind."

"The girl?"

Mareko fixed his father with a hard look. "The resort."

Enele waved a hand. "It is standing, is it not?"

"Of course."

"Then everything will be alright. And if it wasn't standing, we would rebuild. Like after Amos." His father's face screwed up in distaste, the way it always did when the 2016 cyclone came up. Cyclone Amos had ravaged the beach in front of the resort and required rebuilds of four of the deluxe villas.

"It takes more than structural integrity to be successful, Dad."

"There is no success without contentment."

"What's that supposed to mean?"

"Why did Paige leave?"

Mareko slumped back in his chair. "Her holiday was over."

Enele snorted. "Try again, son."

"She was angry with me," Mareko admitted, giving voice to her actions for the first time. "She left because she thinks I used her to get publicity for The Moananui!"

"She is a smart woman. Maybe she is right."

Mareko stiffened. "No, she's fu–no, she's not."

Twenty-nine years and he'd never come so close to swearing in front of his father. Paige's absence was throwing him so far off the rails he'd be lucky to find his way back.

Enele stared at him.

"She's not!"

"Why does she think that?"

"There was a picture of her posted on The Moananui's accounts. She thought I breached her privacy." In truth, it had been Rachel, working up extra marketing materials for the accounts. She'd admitted it as soon as she realised what had happened, but it was too late.

"Have you removed it?"

Mareko hesitated. The image was gone from their social media stream, he'd taken it down immediately. But it wasn't gone from his life. There were plenty of images of Paige on the Internet, but that was the Paige of *One True Love*, not *his* Paige. He still had the original image on his phone, looked at it daily. He'd tried to stop, God knows he'd tried, but every time he'd thought about letting it go, of deleting the evidence of that perfect day they'd shared, his stomach clenched and he thought he might be sick.

"That's not the point. She left me." His hurt soaked the final few words and he flinched, knowing his father could hear it. "Perhaps it is for the best." He said it more to convince himself than his father. "I can't trust someone who leaves when things get tough."

His father laughed. "You think you do not trust her?"

"You think I should?"

"Son," Enele shook his head. "You hired her to watch Rosa for three weeks. Your daughter is the most precious thing in the world to you. If you didn't trust Doctor Beckett, you would never have let her near that girl." He wagged his finger at Mareko. "You are saying this now because you are angry and upset, but that doesn't make it true."

"She thinks I'm in the wrong for trying to protect our family's legacy."

A burst of laughter. "You think The Moananui is our legacy?"

Mareko straightened in his seat.

"Of course it is."

"Ah, my son. You have been gone too long. The white world has filled your head with nonsense." His father reached out and patted Mareko's hand. "This is our legacy. You. Rosa. Family. Love. Those are the things your mother and I wish for you. Not money. Not buildings or land."

"I'm fine," Mareko replied stiffly. "But Rosa–"

His father cut him off. "You want Rosa to inherit a to-do list and unhealthy sleep patterns? Or do you want her to inherit your good heart? The way you care for people? The love you have for your family and your community? Those other things are part of The Moananui, yes. But they are not all The Moananui is. They will remain long after the guests stop and the buildings fall into disrepair." Enele's rough hand squeezed his. "You feel these callouses? My hands are rough because of the work I have spent my life doing at the resort. But when I am called to Heaven, I hope it is not my callouses you remember. I hope it is my love for you. Love is the true legacy we leave behind. Do not throw yours away because you place higher honour on a place than a person."

Mareko reflected on his conversation with his father all the way back to the resort, where he delivered his mother to the spa for her weekly massage treatment before making his way back to the bungalow.

He wandered through the open front door and stopped dead when a familiar voice sounded.

"I don't know, Rosa. I've never tried a souffle. Everything I've heard tells me they're a nightmare to get right."

Lightness filled Mareko's chest. *Paige.*

He burst through Rosa's bedroom door, his eyes scanning the room. She was... not there. Rosa sat on her bed, Penina's phone in her hand.

"Dad?"

"Sorry, lo'u afafine. I should have knocked."

"It's okay." Rosa shifted slightly and Mareko saw Paige then, her heart-shaped face filling the small phone screen. Her hair was scraped back in a stubby ponytail, her face was free of makeup, and even through the grainy image on the screen Mareko had never seen anything so beautiful.

He cleared his throat. "Doctor Beckett." He nodded in acknowledgement, even as every nerve in his body screamed at him to go to her, to snatch the phone out of his daughter's hands and demand she come back to Samoa. Back to him. He'd been a fool, he knew that now, but love made men foolish. That was well-documented.

The thought pulled him up cold and he blinked hard.

*Love?*

*Of course, love,* his father's voice sounded in his head.

He'd suspected, of course. But he'd pushed those feelings aside in the wake of her departure. Now he turned the idea over in his head, and with each memory of Paige that flashed behind his eyes, certainty grew; his heart filling until it felt like his chest might explode.

Heaven help him, he'd been even more blind than he'd first thought.

"Mr Osa," Paige replied, and the coolness of her tone cut across his skin in diamond shards.

He hesitated, before pushing on. "Are... are you well?"

"Quite."

Dear God, this was torture.

"Rosa, do you mind if I speak to Doctor Beckett privately for a moment?"

"I guess. I'll talk to you later, Paige."

"Talk soon, honey."

His daughter slid off the bed, passing him the phone with a suspicious glare, and disappeared. Through the veil of his nerves, Mareko noted that she didn't quite close the door all the way.

"I have an appointment in a few minutes, Mareko. What can I do for you?"

Fear gripped his throat but he persevered.

"I want to apologise face to face."

A beat. Then, "for what?"

"For allowing a picture of you to be posted without your consent. I wasn't the one who posted it, but I am ultimately in charge of our social media accounts so it was my responsibility."

"Who posted it?" Paige's voice was tight, and his heart ached.

"I'm not prepared to reveal that."

"How nice that you get to pick and choose which employees you protect."

"You were never just an employee, Paige. You must know that. You must know how much more you mean to me. To all of us." Before he could help himself, he blurted out "The email I sent, I meant every word."

She opened her mouth, anticipation gripped his throat, and then...

A knock.

"Doctor Beckett?"

Paige's eyes cut to someone he couldn't see off screen and the voice continued. "Mr Baker is here, and his leg looks pretty bad."

"Thanks, Beth." Her eyes found him again and soaked up her image, preserving it in his mind in case this was the last time he ever saw her.

"I have to go," she said softly, and even though he'd been expecting it, his heart sank.

"Of course," he choked out. "It was nice to talk to you."

"You too." Was it him or did her voice sound more fragile than usual as well? "Take care, Mareko."

She ended the call, and he dropped the phone on the bed, desolation settling over him like a blanket.

"Dad?"

"Come in, lo'u afafine."

The mattress dipped where she sat next to him, and the comforting weight of his daughter's head pressed into his chest as she leaned against him.

"I miss her." Rosa's voice was soft but it struck him like a missile. Mareko wrapped his arms around her and pressed a kiss to the silk of her hair.

"So do I," he admitted. "So do I."

OKAY, *Paige. This is it. You can do it.*

Paige shook out her hands, trying to release the nervous energy that had her body wound tighter than a coiled spring. Her heartbeat thundered in her ears, too fast to be healthy, surely. Maybe she should do this later. She could head over to the hospital, borrow an ECG, get checked out and then maybe if she was declared healthy she could come back and try this again.

"Paige!"

*Too late.* Sione stood directly in front of her, his handsome face split by a wide smile.

"You're back!"

"Yeah. Um, I'm looking for Rosa." *You coward*, her internal voice taunted her, and she shook it away. She *was* here for Rosa. Fine, maybe not only Rosa. Her mind had blanked when Mareko had mentioned an email, but she'd gone back through her junk folders and found it. Hidden between ads for mass-produced sweatshop clothes and pills for erectile dysfunction was an email from one Mareko Osa, wherein he declared he was falling for her. He also seemed to mistakenly believe that she was currently with Patrick, but vowed to wait for her, begging her to reach out and put him out of his misery.

Of course, he'd sent that email four weeks ago. Four weeks without contact, while the kindest man she'd known grappled with the knowledge that she'd left him without warning. Just like his late wife.

An email reply would not have sufficed.

Sione nodded. "Of course. They've booked out the Hibiscus Room for her party. I'm on my way there now. Come on." He grabbed her small carryon suitcase and began wheeling it through The Moananui lobby.

Paige trailed behind him, the large, brightly wrapped gift propped up on one hip. This plan had seemed sound a week ago when her mother had suggested it during one of their twice-weekly family therapy sessions, but now that she was here she was doubting the outcome of it. Of course, Paige had found Mareko's email an hour before the session and had been in tears throughout. She would have agreed to anything that she thought might help stopper the well of hurt that burbled inside her.

The therapy, plus an official diagnosis of generalised anxiety disorder and prescription medication for Paige, had seen great strides in her relationship with her parents. So much so that their therapist had recently suggested moving to monthly family sessions, with Paige continuing individually on a fortnightly basis alone while she learnt how to navigate her new reality.

She could never be grateful enough to her father for suggesting it. But she knew now that her gratitude didn't need to manifest into feelings of obligation or guilt to keep her parents happy. Her job was keeping herself happy, and that was why she was back in Samoa.

"Here we are." Sione stopped in front of an open set of whitewashed double doors, plastered with streamers and pictures of Rosa from infancy up.

A smile crept over Paige's face as she studied the pictures on one of the doors. Baby Rosa in the bath, her dark hair spiked up, a gummy smile lighting up her round face. Her first day of school, tall and proud with her too-big backpack in the desert sun. Dressed in a tutu and rain boots with her face painted like a lion on Mareko's shoulders with the Eiffel Tower in the background.

Paige studied the younger Mareko in the picture. His hair was shorter, almost military in style. The crinkles at the corners of his eyes that she loved hadn't yet developed, but he stared up at Rosa with absolute adoration. Paige's heart clenched studying his tender expression. He'd looked at her like that once too. She hoped she wasn't too late to ever see that look again.

"Paige!" Rosa's voice carried across the open space and everyone in attendance spun towards the doors.

Paige shifted from foot to foot, unease prickling at her skin under the weight of so many eyes.

"Malo," she managed, as she was hit by a ten-year-old hurricane that wrapped its arms around her waist and squeezed, knocking the breath from her lungs as she dropped the present she was holding.

"I'm so happy you're here." Rosa buried her face in Paige's ribcage. "I missed you."

"I missed you too, honey." Paige wrapped her arms around the girl's smaller frame. "Happy tenth birthday."

They embraced for a full minute as the party continued on around them, staff toting platters of delicious snacks to groups that chatted or sang gently along to the music of a performance trio in the corner. Paige soaked it in, the feeling of completion. Music, food, and family. Finally, she'd found love. *Her* love. For life. Whatever happened next, she was staying in Samoa. This was where she belonged.

Rosa stood back, but clutched her hand. "I can't believe you came back for my party."

"I wouldn't have missed it for the world." Paige assured her. "Do you want your present now, or later."

"*You* are my present," Rosa declared firmly, and Paige's heart swelled.

"That might be true, but you still need something to unwrap on your birthday." Paige crouched to pick up the large box at her feet. "Here you go." She passed it to Rosa, who immediately sat on the function room floor in her pink puletasi and ripped open the wrapping paper.

"Chef whites?" Rosa's delighted squeal reached the rafters.

"Not only chef whites." Paige sat cross legged on the floor next to her. "There's a lab coat in there. The kind of suit a hotel owner might wear. A bathing suit. A lavalava for kilikiti. And one more thing."

Rosa dug to the bottom of the box, emerging in a mess of white fabric. She held it up and gasped in awe.

"It's amazing."

It was a perfect replica of Anni-Frid's outfit from the Mamma Mia music video, sized to fit a ten-year-old girl. There was a single deviation from authenticity. Like all of the outfits, it had Rosa's name stitched on the left breast area. Kathleen had embroidered them all by hand in the last week while Paige finished up at her practice in New Zealand.

"They're to remind you that you can do anything," Paige said softly, as Rosa stroked the satiny fabric. "Any career you want – any *passion* you have – you can follow it. You can achieve your dreams, whatever they are."

"Fa'afetai lava, Paige." Rosa thanked her, looking up with shining eyes. "I love you."

"I love you, too." Paige smiled through her own tears.

They were cloaked in shadow at that moment, as a figure blocked the light spilling over them.

"Can I see you for a minute, Paige?"

Her stomach twisted. *This.* This moment was why she'd been so nervous. Why she'd already considered turning around and running back to Rotorua innumerable times since she made it to the Auckland International departure lounge.

*No more running.* No matter what Mareko said, her life was here now.

She stood, self-consciously brushing off the back of her light cotton maxi dress. Mareko's blank expression ratcheted her tension higher. Silently, she followed him out of the festive celebration and through the cool corridors to his office. He opened the door for her and she entered, breathing in his scent as she went. The familiar blend of coconut oil, pine and the ocean almost swallowed her whole. Paige stumbled, memories assailing her on all sides, the firm grasp of Mareko's hand on her elbow supporting her as grief and love threatened to overwhelm her. How could she have let this man go? He might have made a mistake, but it was her actions that had broken them. She'd run at the first sign of trouble instead of talking to Mareko, like a fool, and like a fool she'd allowed herself to believe that she could still find happiness while her heart remained with him. Well, stupid games won stupid prizes, and she was being rewarded for it now, trapped in the dark with the man of her dreams, so in love that his very scent knocked her off balance. She righted herself, breathing through her mouth, and entered the room. She couldn't look at him –if she did, her emotions would get the better of her. She needed to be calm for this conversation, ready to accept whatever consequence she faced. Mareko followed her into the office, switching on the lights before leading her to a pair of low turquoise couches by the window. He waited until she sat before taking a seat next to her, and hope lifted her heart at that small gesture.

"These are new," Paige said, running her fingers across the fabric.

"Yes. Rachel had it brought in when she took over the general manager role."

Paige's head shot up. "Rachel is the general manager?"

"She is." Mareko was watching her carefully. "It hasn't been long, but she is doing an excellent job. She knows this place as well as I do and it turned out she was becoming frustrated with the lack of growth opportunities here. When I offered her the position she jumped at it."

"That's fantastic."

Mareko carried on as if she hadn't spoken. "We've also managed to secure a two-year contract with Madison Longley, the travel blogger. She's taking up a part-time position here as our marketing manager starting next month."

*I don't care*, she wanted to yell. *Do you love me?*

"So, what do you do now?"

"We're working that out." For the first time since she'd returned to Samoa, she caught a glimpse of Mareko's smile, tinged with vulnerability. "Something behind the scenes, I think."

"That... that sounds really positive."

"Do you think so?"

"Yes." Paige replied firmly. "It will give you more time with your family. I know Rosa will love that."

"What about you?"

Paige blinked. "What about me?"

Mareko cleared his throat. "Would you like me spending more time with you?"

Paige's heart melted at the uncertainty painted across his strong features. "Oh, Mareko..."

"Please hear me out, Paige." He gripped her hand, twining their fingers together. The familiar sparks shot up her arm, warming her. "I don't know exactly what brought you back to Samoa, but please stay. Stay with me, with Rosa. I know I messed up, that it will take time for you to trust me again. But I'm begging you to give me that time to prove to you that I can be the man you rely on. Let me prove my love to you."

Paige gasped. "You love me?"

"Of course I do. I tried to tell you on the phone last week, but we were interrupted. I wanted everything in place before I returned to New Zealand to convince you. All of these changes are for you. For *us*. I want us to be a family. I know it is asking a lot. If you can't stay, we will still find a way to make it work. My new hours will give me more time to come visit you in New Zealand. We can do long distance until we work out a better plan. I just want to be with you."

"You were coming to New Zealand?"

"My ticket is booked for a flight tomorrow morning. I was coming to tell you I loved you, to swear I will never let anyone hurt you again. I don't care if you're with Patrick, he'll never be what you need. I am, Paige. I can be the man you need. Your husband. The father of your children. It doesn't matter how far you run, I'll follow."

"I won't run again," she swore quickly. "I should have talked to you. I should have trusted you the way you trusted me." Her chest tightened. "I'm sorry."

"Paige Beckett," Mareko went down on his knees in front of the couch, clasping her hand against his chest, "you have nothing to be sorry for. Your reactions are your own, and you are perfect for me the way that you are. Since you arrived at The Moananui, you have spread sunshine throughout every inch of it. Throughout every inch of me," he corrected. "I was living in the dark for so long. It took you to show me the light. Please, lo'u alofa. Please come back to me."

Tears streamed down Paige's face and she wiped them hastily away with her free hand.

"I already have," she managed. "I've moved here. I'm not going back to New Zealand."

Mareko's eyes brightened. "You're not?"

She shook her head. "Not for two years, at least. I've got a visa to work here until then. I've already shipped my stuff." It had been a frantic week since she showed up at therapy in tears after her video call with Rosa and Mareko. Planning, packing, paperwork. She'd even had to use her minor celebrity status to get her visa application expedited.

"You won't need a work visa by then," Mareko said, gruffly. "I'm never letting you go again."

"You'll never need to," Paige assured him. "I've been running away from my problems all my life instead of facing them head on. I did it when I was younger by avoiding conflict with my parents, and then by literally running. Away from my wedding, which turned out to be the best decision of my life. But then when things got too much with you, I ran then as well."

"You were right to be angry."

"But not to leave you. When you love someone the way I love you, you don't leave when things get tough. You work through them together. I need to be better at that."

"You will be, lo'u alofa. You can achieve any goal you set your mind to."

"I'm glad you think so," Paige smiled. "Because right now my major priority is being the best partner to you and friend to Rosa that I can be."

"Oh, Paige," Mareko swore, crushing her to his chest and peppering her hair with kisses. "You already are."

# EPILOGUE

 *ne year later*

MAREKO SIPPED his 'ava and stared out at the ocean. In a fiery show of colours, the sun dipped below the horizon, orange and pink and purple slashed across the sky in the haphazard streaks of Nature's paintbrush.

Soft hands slid around his waist, dipping under the loose cotton shirt he wore, and as the Southern Cross twinkled in the inky blue of the approaching night, his wife pressed her lips to his neck

"Are you thinking heavy thoughts, lo'u alofa?"

Mareko smiled, covering Paige's linked fingers with a hand of his own.

"Leai, l'ou alofa. I am reflecting on how lucky I am."

"Ah." She rested her chin on his shoulder and stared out towards the ocean with him. The palm trees separating the bungalow from the beach swayed gently, their fronds moving in a lazy to-and-fro as the night breeze whispered promises across the island.

*This day is done. A new one dawns tomorrow.*

This had always been Mareko's favourite time of the day – the slow moments when the work was done and evening became night. He had missed so many of these twilight hours in the past, too buried in his work and his own ideas of success to look up and notice how quickly each day faded, and how the sun rose again promising new beginnings.

This night was his favourite. Just as the night before had been, and the night before that. Any night he wound up sitting on the porch of his childhood home with his daughter safely asleep inside and his brilliant wife in his embrace was his favourite. He was blessed that he'd had so many of them thus far. He fervently hoped the tradition would continue far into the future. Although, some things might change.

Reaching behind him, he caressed Paige's stomach, which swelled under her dress. Their son was due in two months, and he couldn't be happier. Rosa was thrilled to be a big sister and had already made an ABBA-heavy playlist for Paige's labour. Both sets of grandparents had wept with joy when they'd shared the positive results of their early scan at their wedding six months earlier.

Unlike his first wedding, his parents had been in attendance when he and Paige married on the beach in front of the resort at sunset. So had hers, Kathleen and Gregory embracing him fiercely following the vows, proud tears shining in their eyes. Rachel had taken time from her busy day managing The Moananui to officiate their ceremony, and Rosa had escorted Paige down the sandy aisle. But

Mareko only had eyes for his bride. Clad in a simple white silk tank top and flowing organza skirt, her silvery hair loose around her shoulders and a pink hibiscus flower behind her ear, Paige had joined her hands with his under the simple wooden arch and bound their lives together even more fully.

Afterwards, they sat with their family on the porch where they'd shared their first kiss –where they stood now – and under a sparkling canopy of fairy lights they'd shared a meal from the resort kitchen before slicing into the wedding cake Rosa had lovingly created. Since then, nothing compared to nights on his porch with Paige. This was Mareko's heaven. The resort was flourishing under Rachel's leadership, leaving Mareko a comfortable nine-to-five role as Chief Financial Officer. He was able to sneak away during the day to catch lunch with his wife, or watch Rosa's swimming competitions and dance performances at school. His mother had moved into the retirement village with his father soon after Paige's return to Samoa, citing a desire to spend more time with Enele, wherever that might be.

Life was good. For too long he had hustled, chasing some arbitrary dream of success. Now, he could see prosperity every time he looked around. Could reach out and touch it, with every stroke of Rosa's hair, every caress of Paige's stomach, every press of his lips against her cheek.

"Rosa is asleep," Paige whispered in his ear. "She's worn out. Iosefa's challenge for her to master eclairs has her brain working overtime."

Mareko swelled with pride. "She is incredible."

"She certainly is."

The two of them had sat down with Rosa and clearly explained that there was no expectation that she would take over the resort when she was older, that they wanted her to follow her own passions. It turned out though, that in her quest to find a resort-marketable skill, Rosa had fallen in love with desserts. At least once a week Mareko came home from work to find music blasting through the bungalow while Rosa whipped up some fantastic creation. Her love of being in the kitchen had sparked his own interest in cooking, and with his reduced hours he took great pleasure in cooking meals for his family most nights, experimenting with recipes and perfecting the traditional dishes of his youth. Most nights he and Rosa worked side-by-side to prepare the evening meal, talking about their days until Paige returned from the hospital and they carried the dishes out to the porch to eat in the fading light of day.

"Thank you," Paige said suddenly behind him, and Mareko twisted in his seat to look up at her.

"For what, lo'u alofa?"

"For everything. For supporting me. Loving me. Building a family with me."

"Ah, Paige." Mareko pulled her around the chair and across his lap, cradling her close to him. "You know better than that. This family was bound by blood before you arrived, but it is you who has made us whole. Not because of the role you play, but because of who you are. We are happier, stronger because of you. *I* am better because of you."

"I'm better because of you, too," his wife murmured, pressing a kiss against his jawline.

Mareko's blood stirred. This woman. Would she never stop undoing him? Would he never stop wanting her, craving her, turning his world sideways to please her?

*Never,* he vowed silently.

"Can we go inside, please?" Paige trailed her lips along the column of his neck. "Tonight is the first night of my maternity leave, and I'd like to celebrate with my husband."

"Anything for you," Mareko growled, standing upright, cradling her against his chest. Paige squealed out a laugh, clutching at him as he strode inside, his drink and the sunset outside forgotten.

Mareko deposited Paige gently onto their bed, her blonde hair fanning out like a halo on the pillow, her peach scent teasing him as she reached up to twine her arms around his neck, their lips meeting in a passionate kiss.

Mareko might have spent most of his life on a tropical island, but this?

This was paradise.

THE END.

# ABOUT THE AUTHOR

Award winning author Courtney Clark Michaels has been reading and writing romance since she first pilfered a novel out of her mother's bedroom at the tender age of thirteen. While her newly discovered writing hobby didn't endear her to her teachers, it did make Maths more interesting for her friends. Ironically, after gaining degrees in Criminology and English, Courtney now teaches high school students and spends a fair bit of time bemoaning their off-task behaviour. Karma is indeed a bitch. Courtney's passion for writing strong, independent heroines and smart, sexy men is equal only to her passions for travel, online shopping and patting other people's dogs. She is lucky enough to live in the heart of New Zealand's winemaking region with her own alpha man, a few gorgeous children and a hyperactive poochon named Kevin.

# MORE BY CCM

Pacific Passions Series
Pregnant by the Prince
Rooming With Royalty
Protecting His Princess
Christmas in Paradise
Ginger Kisses

Hot Rugby Knights Series
Game Changer
Off His Game

Sign up for my free newsletter at my website: www.courtneyclarkmichaels.com for updates, giveaways and exclusive content.

www.ingramcontent.com/pod-product-compliance
Lightning Source LLC
Chambersburg PA
CBHW020656120726
47906CB00001B/295